Sand Rabbit Murders

A Brick North Mystery

by Augustine Meijer

Also by Augustine Meijer

Who were the Sand Rabbits?

Having been invited by Catherine the Great to Russia because Germans were hard workers, then ordered to leave the country by the Tsar with nothing because they were German and couldn't be trusted. Homeless, they searched for a place to belong. But, where could they go? With help from family members who had immigrated earlier, many came to St. Joseph, Michigan. They rented the most affordable housing they could find; homes built on the lakefront. Here they would be safe and could raise their children. They would become known as "Sand Rabbits." Originally a derogatory label applied by the well-to-do, it eventually was worn a badge-of-honor by those who lived there.

IMMIGRANTS

At the turn of the 20th century when the great migration from Europe was taking place, many Germans from colonies located in Russia, and other areas of Europe, left their homes and some of them settled in Southwest Michigan. The original houses in this beach area were home to a large number of them. They had a strong work ethic, religious beliefs and customs which they passed on to their children who were sometimes affectionately called "Sand Rabbits" by locals. These immigrants easily adapted to the American culture. They made a great contribution to this community and to all of Southwest Michigan.

This book is dedicated to the men and women of law enforcement. In small villages and giant metropolises, those who wear a badge put aside their problems, step beyond their limitations, and find a way to make our communities better places to live. A sincere thank you to those with whom I have worked and who became de facto beta-readers.

Finally, with love to my wife, who has put up with me writing into the wee hours as I struggle to get thoughts onto paper.

Sand Rabbit Murders

Chapter 1

North handed the forty-five hundred dollar check to the agent. It was the largest check he had ever written. He had also just broken the promise he'd made to himself that he would never buy a house. But, here he was, being handed the keys to a two-bedroom bungalow on the lakefront.

After his discharge from the army, North had spent years living in boarding houses. After tiring of boarding houses, he lived in the Swanson Hotel for two years, which offered only slightly more privacy. Months of living in his parent's cottage in Hell changed his mind about homeownership. Having a private bathroom and a kitchen was better than he had imagined.

Vine Street was below the bluff that overlooked Lake Michigan. The houses were predominately occupied by factory and shop workers. Like most the other homes in the area, his place was built on a shallow foundation situated upon the white sands for which Lake Michigan was famous. His property backed up to the tracks; freight and passenger trains rumbled past throughout the day and night.

With some used furniture in place, North set up residence. The cat that had adopted him while in Hell made himself at home. Having investigated every room and closet, Gatto called dibs on the overstuffed chair in the living room. From his perch on the back of the chair, he could sun himself and keep an eye on the comings and goings through the neighborhood. He seemed most interested in the children who made their way to the stairs that led up the bluff and to their school.

A few blocks from North's new home was the Silver Beach Amusement Park, closed now for the winter. The most imposing feature of the area was the empty factory that had been the Cooper Wells Hosiery Company. The three- and four-story Cooper Wells buildings had been vacant since fifty-two when the factory closed. Pigeons and vagrants occupied spaces where knitting machines once churned out socks and stockings. During the Second World War, production was devoted to the war effort when parachutes and green wool socks were churned out in quantities no one could have imagined.

North had been back in LaSalle Harbor for nearly four weeks before he knocked on the Chief of Police's door. Pete Cummings looked up from a stack of reports he was authorizing, "North! I was beginning to wonder if you were planning on coming back." The chief stuck out a hand which Brick shook. "Damn sorry to hear about Miss Kingston. I didn't know you two were close until Tiffin told me."

North nodded, "Thanks. I didn't know how close we were until she…" he paused for a moment, "until she was gone."

"You doing okay?" Cummings was genuinely concerned.

North reached into his jacket pocket and pulled out a pack of Pall Malls, and lit a cigarette, "If I've learned anything in life, it's that people die."

"That doesn't make a loss any less difficult."

"No," North took a pull on the cigarette and blew smoke toward the ceiling lamp before he continued, "it just means that I've got to get used to the world the way it is and not the way I want it to be." He looked over his shoulder and into the squad room. "Where is Tiff anyway?"

"He and Uher took a call. Workers found remains down at the old Cooper Wells building. It looks like the body has been there a while." Cumming drew flame into the moist tobacco in his pipe, "So," he sucked on the stem of the pipe, "you coming back to work, or just stopping by for a social?"

"It's about time that I get back to work," there was neither joy nor disdain in his voice. "What do you have for me?"

"First, you'll want these," Cummings reached into his desk and pulled out the badge and revolver that North relinquished when he had been placed on leave several months prior. "Grab a desk and spend some time going over the blotter. Get yourself caught up; it's been a busy winter so far."

"Grab a desk? What's wrong with my old desk?"

"Uher has been using it since I teamed him up with Tiffin. You can use Uher's old desk."

North pursed his lips and nodded, "Okay, Chief." He walked into the squad room and looked at the desk in which Dan Uher used to sit. It was identical to the one North had previously occupied. He walked across the room, grabbed a metal coat rack, and placed it next to the desk. On this, he hung both his suit jacket and the new grey fedora he had purchased to replace the brown Bradmore that he had worn for years. There was much he was going to have to get used to.

He had just finished going through files of the open cases when Tiffin and Uher came up the stairs. It was a full minute before either of them noticed the occupant of the desk in the corner, "Brick?!" Tiffin said as he crossed the twenty-five-foot distance in just a couple of strides. "When did you get here?" North stood as his former partner approached. Instead of the expected handshake, Tiffin grabbed his right hand and pulled himself in for an awkward hug.

Looking over his shoulder at Uher, Tiffin said, "You don't know how good it is to have you back."

3

"I'll try not to take that personally," Uher glared.

"Kaye's been worried about you," Tiffin continued. "I know she's going to want to see you."

North sat down and resumed his study of the blotter, "Tell her maybe soon."

"Where are you staying?" Tiffin asked as he lit a cigarette.

"Bought a house down on Vine Street."

"You bought a house. Thought you didn't want to be tied down with a mortgage?"

"I didn't."

"Wait. You didn't buy a house, or you didn't get a mortgage?"

"Long story. What are you and Dan working on?" North motioned for Tiffin to sit.

"Whirlpool has purchased the Cooper Wells factory. They're remodeling one of the buildings for some research center."

"And…?"

"And, a construction crew found the remains of a girl behind one of the boilers they were removing."

North looked up, "Girl? How old?"

"Doc Howard," Tiffin referred to the county coroner, "says the girl was probably in her mid-teens."

"Any idea of how long she was there?"

"According to the doc, she could have been there four or more years."

"So maybe right after the factory shut down?"

4

Tiffin nodded, "That'd be my guess. A body stuffed behind a boiler would undoubtedly get some attention if the boiler operators were still around."

North lit a cigarette, "So after the plant closed. That's still a lot of water over the dam."

"She had dark hair and was wearing a white blouse and a yellow and white striped jumper. Not much to go on."

North agreed, "You guys check missing persons yet?"

Tiffin looked at Uher, who was listening to their conversation, "We're all over that, right Dan?"

"Oh, yeah. I'm on it." Uher said as he stood and walked to a file cabinet.

"So, Brick, how are you doing?" Tiffin's tone was sincere.

"I'm okay. I'd rather not talk about it." North lit another cigarette. The one he had just lighted moments before smoldered in the ashtray.

Tiffin made a note of the two cigarettes burning, "Yeah, I can see you're okay." He changed the subject, "So, does the chief have you working on anything?"

"Not yet. He suggested I read the blotter and get a feel for what's been going on."

"Typical holiday season. Caught a ring of thieves that were breaking into houses stealing Christmas gifts. They were gypsies. They're spending the holidays in the county jail; the judge thinks they're a flight risk."

"Anything more exciting than that?"

"Two bank robberies, a few stolen cars, and a prostitution ring that we shut down." Tiffin paused to think, "Oh, and the Sheriff, District Attorney, and several Councilmen were all indicted for corruption."

North smiled, "Yeah, I heard about that."

Chief Cummings walked into the squad room, "North, grab a uni and head down to the Tin City migrant camp. The manager just found the body of a man in the pump house."

"On it, Chief," North grabbed his coat and hat. On standing, Tiffin took note of the scar on the back of Brick's head.

"Holy shit, what happened to you?"

"Used my head to stop an ax," North said as he pushed the grey Stetson Stratosphere over the scar.

"How's the ax?" Tiffin joked.

North used his head to point between Tiffin and Uher, "You two using the car?"

"Not at the moment," Tiffin responded.

"Uher," North teased, "you let Tiff here answer all the questions?"

"Well, he is my nanny."

"Okay, someone will explain that to me later." North grabbed the phone and was immediately connected to the switchboard, "This is Detective North. I'll be going to the Tin City camp."

"Thank you, detective, and we're all so sorry about what happened to Sylvia."

Not knowing what to say, North put the receiver down onto the phone's cradle. On the first floor, he stopped at the Sergeant's desk, "Hey, Higdon. Who've you got that can take a ride with me down to Tin City?"

"Well, hello to you, too, Brick." The duty sergeant looked at his roster. "Davis is here. You can take him."

6

North had worked with Officer Gerald Davis a few times before. He was someone that North knew would move up in the ranks. Higdon picked up the phone, "Connect me with the locker room." A moment passed, "Is Davis back there? Okay, tell him I need to see him pronto." Two minutes later, Davis appeared, adjusting his Sam Browne as he walked.

"Detective North. It's good to see you, sir!" Officer Gerald Davis was in his early twenties, tall, thin, and impeccably groomed.

"Davis. How's Sergeant Higdon been treating you?"

"Oh, very well, sir. The Sergeant is a good leader." North was sure he saw a blush under Davis's dark brown skin.

They checked the Ford Mainline the detective squad shared out from the motor pool and turned toward the river and the migrant camp the locals called 'Tin City' because of the tin-roofed shacks that housed migrant fruit pickers from May until October. Some of the shacks were set up as bunkhouses for single men. Others accommodated families. Few of them had running water, and even fewer had electricity. But, they were cheap to rent, which allowed the laborers to keep more of their hard-earned, but measly income.

The elderly labor camp manager met them as they arrived, "Glad you could be troubled to come out. It's been almost an hour since I called."

North didn't take the bait, "Where's the body, mister…?"

"Fuchs, Harry Fuchs."

"Okay, Mister Fuchs, where's the body?"

The man pointed a shaky finger toward a small brick building near the back of the camp, "There in the pump house."

North continued to ask questions as they walked, "Do you know the victim?"

"Hell yes, I know who it is. It's Mack Cudlip."

The detective added to the notes he was taking, "Cudlip his name, or just what people call him?"

"How the Hell would I know that. It's what he said his name was."

"Mack his first name or a nickname?"

The old man stopped, "Son, I'm gonna be eighty-one come May. I never met no fool ask so many questions as you."

As they approached the pump house, North could make out a pair of well-worn leather boots sticking out from the door. A few yards further on, he saw the entire body stretched out face first on the building's concrete floor.

North lit a cigarette. "I know how much you like a good question," he said sarcastically. "Is this how you found him?"

Fuchs stared between North and the officer for a moment, "No, I found him sipping tea and eating cake. Of course, this is how I found him."

North stooped down and examined the body. The left side of its skull was crushed. Dried blood mixed with the dust beneath the corpse. "Davis, wait out at the road for Doc Howard."

"Yes, sir," the officer took off at a trot.

"Anyone have a problem with Cudlip?" North took a drag on the Pall Mall.

"Everybody has a problem with somebody. I doubt that it was any different for him."

North's tone revealed his frustration, "Let me change that question. Do you know of anyone, in particular, that had a problem with the deceased?"

"Well, you may as well know; I had a problem with him," Fuchs was matter-in-fact in his response.

8

"What kind of problem did you have?"

"Cudlip was always behind on his rent. I kicked him out of the shanty he was set up in."

North's pencil hovered above his notepad, "When did you do that?"

"Last night. Probably about half-past eight. I told him that he couldn't keep staying here without paying up."

"Did he leave?"

"Yeah, he wondered up Britain Avenue. I watched him for a few minutes, then went back to my place."

"So, you might have been the last person to see Cudlip alive. Is that what you're telling me?"

Fuchs became defensive, "How the heck should I know who saw him after I did?"

"Tell you what," North picked a piece of tobacco off his lip, "I may have more questions for you. Don't think about going anywhere."

"Where would I go? I'm eighty years old and work here to keep a roof over my head," Fuchs wandered toward the building that served as the camp's kitchen during the peak season.

Davis led the coroner up to the pump house. "Brick!" Doctor Howard shouted when he was about thirty feet away, "I'm glad you're back!"

North shouted back, "Good to see you too, Mel. How has the world been treating you?"

"The world?" Howard paused to think, "The world treats me like the idiot cousin at a family reunion. I get invited to the party, but no one wants to talk to me."

North chuckled, "The problem of working with the dead, huh?"

9

The doctor rubbed his thumbs against his fingers, "I guess they don't know that death doesn't rub off. So, what have you got?"

North pointed to the body, "Meet my new friend. Someone decided to bash his skull in."

Howard lowered himself down onto a knee next to the corpse, "I'll know more when I get him back to the morgue, but it definitely looks like blunt-force trauma. Do you know who this was?"

"I'm told that his name was Mack Cudlip. I'll run the name when I get back to the office and see what we can learn about him."

Chapter 2

Tiffin took a bite out of his hamburger and wiped his mouth with a paper napkin. He looked at North, who was sipping a beer, "Okay, tell me, how is it that you used your head to stop an ax?"

North grimaced at the memory, "Somebody took up residence in my cottage and took offense to my wanting him out."

"And he hit you in the head with an ax?" Tiffin took another bite of his burger.

"That's the short answer," North held an empty shot glass over his head. Roxy, the self-described 'big old friendly gal' and co-owner of the Trophy Room, laid another shot of whiskey in front of him and took the empty from his hand.

"What's the long answer?"

"He was hiding from a manhunt," North took a sip of the whiskey. "He'd raped and murdered at least three women that we knew of."

"And he hid from you in your cottage?" Tiffin asked incredulously.

"He didn't know it was my cottage. It was just an open door."

"I joke about your hard head, but how is it that he didn't kill you?"

"My old Bradmore caused the ax to slip. Damn hat saved my life."

"I'd say that you're lucky to be alive."

"That seems to be the general consensus."

Tiffin finished the burger and took a sip of the beer in front of him, "Alright, what's with you buying a house? You left me with the impression that you'd never do that."

North smiled, "I got used to having a private bath and a kitchen in my months in the cottage. It was hard to imagine going back to a shared can."

"So, where's the house?"

"Seven hundred block of Vine. It's a single-story, two-bedroom."

"So, suddenly you're a Sand Rabbit, are you?" Tiffin sniggered.

"Yeah, I guess I am."

"Did you mean it when you said you didn't get a mortgage? How'd you manage to do that?"

"My folks left me enough money to buy the house," North finished his beer.

Tiffin laughed, "So, I'm sitting at a table with Daddy Warbucks. I'll let you pay for my lunch."

"Okay, Orphan Annie," North grinned, "what did Uher dig up on Mack Cudlip?"

Tiffin flipped open his notepad, "Byron Mack Cudlip has been arrested twenty-seven times in LaSalle Harbor since nineteen forty-four. All for public drunkenness or petty theft."

"Is he from Michigan, or has he been a traveler?" North lit a cigarette.

Tiffin referred to the notepad, "Originally, Harrisburg, Pennsylvania. But he's a transient that's been just about everywhere between the Appalachians and the Mississippi."

North nodded, "So, he's been a busy man."

"Yeah, busy being a leech on society."

"Ha! Kind of like you letting me pay for your lunch," North chuckled.

"Thanks! I told you that Kaye is expecting again, didn't I? I've got to save every penny I can."

A surprised look came to North, "No, you didn't." Then, not knowing what to say, he added, "Good for you." North stood, crushed the Stetson onto his head, and walked to the bar. He handed Roxy three dollars, "Keep the change."

"Thanks, Brick. And hey, good to see you back. I almost started to miss you," Roxy kidded.

"You know if you weren't married...."

The big gal blushed, "You're a tease."

Back at the safety building, North called the FBI in Detroit. Cudlip had stayed under their radar. While he was making that call, Tiffin was digging through blotters going back several months, "That pump house where the body was found has been a popular place."

"How's that?" North lit a cigarette and leaned back in the chair.

"It's a well-liked place for vagrants to spend the night. Your friend Cudlip was arrested just last month for drunkenness with two other men right there."

"So, he gets kicked out of Tin City and decides to squat in the pump house." North sat upright, "Who were the others with him?"

"Let me see," Tiffin checked his notes, "Alvin Pates originally out of Biloxi, Mississippi, and James Lewis, originally from Kansas City, Missouri."

"Great," North took a pull on the cigarette, "transients are always so easy to track down."

"Uher and I are heading over to the morgue to see if Doc Howard can tell us anything about the girl that was found. You want me to see if he has anything on Cudlip yet?"

"Sure. That'd be great. I'm going to head back down to Tin City and see if Fuchs can tell me anything about Pates and Lewis."

Sargeant Higdon freed up officer Artie Davidson to go with North. Davidson drove one of the department's black and white's while the detective read through his notes. Tin City was in the area that LaSalle Harbor residents referred to as the flat's, the former flood plain of the river before it was dammed upstream. They were there in the amount of time it took North to smoke a cigarette. A few older men were gathered outside the kitchen chatting. They got quiet as the police car pulled up.

"Any of you know I can find Fuchs?" North said as he stepped out of the car.

One of the men spat, "Don't give a fuck about Fuchs." The others laughed.

"If you're done with your poetry, why don't you tell me where I can find him." North lit a cigarette and held the pack out to the poet, who greedily pulled two out of the red package.

"He's in the kitchen."

"See, that wasn't so hard." North turned to Davidson, "Keep an eye on this lot while I go talk to Fuchs."

"Yes, sir," he replied. With his hand on his nightstick, he turned to the transients, "Why don't you gents give me your names. Just so I know who I'm babysitting."

North pushed his way through the screen door and into the dining hall. Eight tables that amounted to little more than saw horses with one by sixes stretched between them filled the space. Around each table were ten mismatched chairs. Even empty, the room smelled of rotting food, cigarette smoke, and unwashed people. He heard the sound of someone moving around behind a partition on the narrow end of the room, "Fuchs! You back there?"

"Who wants to know?!"

"Detective North, we spoke this morning," North added his own cigarette smoke to the ambiance of the room.

"You're just gonna be a thorn in my side, ain't you?" Fuchs grumbled as he walked around the wooden partition.

"I'm looking to see if you know either Alvin Pates or James Lewis. They were arrested with Cudlip back in November after being rounded up in the pump house for drunkenness."

Fuchs wiped his hands on the towel he was holding before tossing it onto one of the tables, "Pates? He's around when he can pay the rent. If he's doing good, he pays a week's rent for Cudlip."

"So, why would they be sleeping off a drunk in the pump house if they usually flop here?"

Fuchs pointed to a handwritten sign on the wall. It read in part, "Rent: Bunkhouse $1/week, Cabin $3/week, Meals 15¢/plate. Rent is due on Friday. NO ALCOHOL."

"So, if they show up drunk…." North started.

"They get their asses kicked out. I don't abide drunkards or gamblers."

15

"How about this James Lewis. You know him?"

"Don't know no Lewis. But there's always men coming by trying to get a free meal or a place to flop. Maybe he'd be someone I'd sent packing."

North looked at the elderly man, "When's the last time your saw Pates?"

"Don't rightly know. Maybe a week, maybe more."

"Where would he go?"

"How the Sam Hill would I know? Maybe you ought to ask some of the floaters that hang around looking for handouts."

North took a final drag on his cigarette before crushing it under his toe, "Like some of the men outside?"

"See, you're smarter than you look!" Fuchs picked up the towel, "Now, I got work to do." He walked back behind the partition.

Davidson was chatting with the men that North had left him with. He thanked the men for their time and followed the detective back to the radio car. "You learn anything from them?" North asked as he slipped into the passenger seat.

"Got their names. They're all transients. None of them are local."

"Thanks, Artie. Why don't you run me by Turner's Smoke Shop on our way back." North stared out the window as Davidson steered the car up the hill and the smoke shop.

"I hear they've broken ground for a shopping center out on Napier. That's going to put some stress on the businesses downtown," Davidson made small talk.

North shook his head, "Artie, I don't see some out-of-the-way shopping plaza hurting business in town."

16

"Well, I hear that shopping centers are going great guns back east."

Tiffin and Uher pulled up to the back doors of Memorial Hospital. One level down from the main entrance and backing up to the river, the morgue was just inside. They found Doc Howard sitting at a small desk writing notes. The skeletal remains of a young girl were spread out on the examination table. He looked up from the notepad, "Oh, hey Tiff, Uher."

Tiffin looked at the remains, "What can you tell us about our Jane Doe?"

"Probably not as much as you'd like," the doctor rose and walked to the exam table. "Based on the shape of the skull, I'd say we have a Cacausoid subadult female. As canines, premolars, and second molars emerge between ten and twelve years of age, in my professional opinion, she was between fourteen and sixteen. I'd put her at approximately 165 centimeters, or five feet, five inches."

"So, no cause of death?" Tiffin lit a cigarette and handed the pack to Uher, who had his hand out.

"There's no visible sign of trauma to the skeletal remains. What little bit of flesh that endured doesn't give me anything to go on."

"So, we've got a five-and-a-half-foot-tall brunette female of about fifteen. Anything that'd help us identify her, doc?" Tiffin spoke as he scratched notes on his pad.

"Nothing unusual about what she was wearing. Summer-weight cotton dress, yellow and white stripes. She wore no jewelry and had no shoes. Simple cotton panties and a Maidenform bra completed her list of clothing."

Tiffin thought for a moment, "Okay, fifteen-year-old killed during the summer months based on her clothing. How long would it take for a body to become this decomposed?"

Doc Howard paused to think, "There's a lot of variables to consider. But best guess? Four or five years; maybe less."

"Anything else, doc?" Uher asked.

"Oh, there is one thing. Miss Doe presents with *diastema*."

The two detectives looked at each other; Doc Howard pointed at the front teeth on the skull, "This gap between the two front teeth is called diastema."

Tiffin looked up from the skull and to the coroner, "How is that helpful?"

"It's a hereditary and dominant trait. If she has it, there's almost a one hundred percent chance that one of her parents has it."

Nodding his understanding, Tiffin looked to the bank of refrigerated cabinets on the far wall, "Is Mr. Cudlip a resident of one of those?"

"Indeed," Doc Howard began, "the late Mr. Cudlip is a guest."

"Have you had a chance to examine him yet?"

The doctor shook his head, "Only superficially. It'll be late tonight or tomorrow before I'll get a chance to do a thorough examination."

"Okay. Call when you get something."

"Always do, Barry. Always do," Howard said as he sat back at his desk to continue to work on his notes.

While Uher and Tiffin made their way back to the Safety Building, North continued searching for Pates and seeing if anyone knew James Lewis. The afternoon took Davidson and him through many of the shabbier areas of LaSalle Harbor. They spent considerable time at the ship canal talking with the transients seeking work on the docks and warehouses.

North walked into the squad room just as the sun was setting. A glance at the clock showed it to be a quarter after five. "What do you think, Tiff?" He said as he slid a chair up next to his former partner's desk.

"I think I've spent a day being busy but getting nowhere."

"Feel the same way. It seems that Alvin Pates is a ghost. And other than the arresting officer, no one has ever seen James Lewis."

Tiffin stood and pulled his suit jacket off the back of the chair, "Well, I'm going to go home and see what Kaye has for dinner. What are you up to tonight?"

"Don't know. Probably hang around here for a while and catch up with what's been going on."

"If I know Kaye," Tiffin paused to light a cigarette, "she's made plenty to eat. Why don't you come home with me and get a homecooked meal?"

"Thanks, but I think I'll pass." North stood and walked over to the desk he was using. He thought a little harder about the offer, "Tell Kaye that I'd be happy to come over one of these nights."

Tiffin smiled, "Good! I'll tell her." He picked up his hat and headed for the stairs, "'Night Brick. Glad you're back."

North spent several hours going through the blotter and reading associated files. It wasn't until the cleaning crew came through to pick up the trash that he finally left the office.

There were few street lights in his new neighborhood. In the middle of the block, his house was only illuminated by the light coming from neighboring homes. He was greeted with a familiar 'mew' as he stepped onto the porch, "Okay, cat. Let me get in the door before you get bossy."

He pushed the upper of two buttons on a brass plate by the door, causing the light over the kitchen to come on. North hung his suit,

19

washed up, and poured a shot of bourbon before he put a plate of food down for Gatto. "Eat up, you little freeloader." For himself, North pulled the key from the top of a can of Spam. After a half minute of turning the key, the lid was free. He cut two slices of the pink meat and tossed them into a frying pan. As they sizzled, he widgeted a can of pork and beans open and threw them into a saucepan. The silence of his meal was broken only by the sound of the cat purring as it cleaned itself.

After cleaning up from his dinner, he sat in the living room, sipping bourbon. The only light was from the radio dial, tuned to the new radio station broadcasting from a studio and tower on Industrial Island.

North fell asleep sitting in the overstuffed chair; the cat curled up at his thigh. He awoke with a start to the sound of static after the radio station had signed off for the night. His thoughts were transported thirteen years into the past. He found himself in the Ardene Forest, trying to desperately get a damaged SCR-300 backpack radio to work, "Sergeant North, 99th Infantry to HQ, over. North, 99th Infantry to HQ, come in HQ, over." The SCR-300 held eighteen vacuum tubes. If even one of those were damaged, it could mean that HQ could hear him, but he couldn't hear their response or that he wasn't broadcasting at all.

The ever-changing front had left him separated from his unit and out of ammunition. Finding a deceased signalman and radio gave a glimmer of hope. At least until he found the radio was as dead as the man on whose back it was strapped. "Shit," North whispered to himself as he scavenged the signalman's pockets for anything he could use. A partial pack of smokes and some M&Ms from a ration kit were all he could find. He ate the candy and pushed the cigarettes into his breast pocket before crawling back into the bush.

"Leutnant!" a German voice shouted. *"Ich höre etwas!"* "Lieutenant! I hear something! Another voice responded, *"Was hörst du?"* "What did you hear?"

20

"Pssst, hör zu." "Shhh, listen." The German troops fell silent. North held his breath.

"It is nothing," the Lieutenant finally said. "Just the imagination of a soldier who is too young to be away from his mother's breast." The other soldiers laughed as they proceeded away from where North had hidden.

The walkie-talkie chirped, "Brick? Brick, are you there? I can't find you, Brick." It was Sylvia's voice. He crawled back to the radio, held the headset to his ear, and squeezed the talk button, "Syl! I'm here!" he shouted. "Brick, are you there? Please, I can't find you. Where are you?" Again and again, he keyed the microphone and called out to her. His call was met with only static.

Chapter 3

T he December wind blowing in off Lake Michigan cut through the dungarees and Mackinaw that North had donned. He had coaxed the cat out the front door as he began his walk; it was just past one in the morning. After almost losing his new hat to the wind, he had turned back to the house within a half-hour. Gatto was waiting for him when he returned. "Couldn't take the weather either, huh bub?"

North pulled off his outerwear and boots before falling back onto the bed. His brain acknowledged the freight train that barreled past the back of his house. He made a mental note to push the glasses and plates that would have rattled themselves forward from the vibrations of the train, further back into the cabinets in the morning.

Four inches of snow greeted him when he stepped out of the house's side door at half-past seven. The sun wouldn't be up for another forty minutes. With the heavy clouds blocking the moon and the general lack of street lights, North's thought about walking to the Safety Building quickly evaporated.

He fumbled for the key to the pickup and climbed in. The engine turned over slowly. "The oil must be as thick as tar," he thought to himself as he willed the flathead six to start. He was just beginning to lose hope when the engine fired up. He lit a cigarette and smoked while the truck warmed up. The Dodge made its way slowly toward Water Street, which would take him up the bluff. He was amazed to see children climbing the seventy-three concrete steps up the bluff to their school. He smiled at the memory of walking in the snow to school during winters growing up in Wolverine.

North found a parking spot near the Fifth Wheel Diner. The wind coming in off the lake was brutal, and the warmth of the diner was welcome. A young waitress whom he had not seen since his trip to Hell poured a cup of coffee for him the moment he sat down at the counter. "Anything else this morning, detective?"

Brick smiled, "What do you recommend?"

She thought for a moment, "I'd recommend the steak and eggs with a side of toast."

He took a sip of the coffee, "Because it's so good or it's the most expensive thing on the menu?"

"Well," she paused, "the boss said to push it. But a big man like you could use a hearty breakfast. Especially on a morning like this."

North took a swallow of the coffee, "Okay, you sold me. Steak very rare, eggs over hard, and dry toast."

She turned to the service window and yelled back, "Elmer bleeding, flop a couple hard, and dough with no cow paste."

He was just opening the paper he had picked up on the way in when she turned back, placed her elbows on the counter, and gave North a view down the front of her pink uniform, "I haven't seen you for a long time. I was beginning to worry that you'd found someplace else for breakfast."

"Well, doll," he took another swig of the coffee, "for a while, I did."

She smiled, shook her head, and stepped down the counter to serve another customer.

In his customary fashion, he inhaled his breakfast, cleaned the plate with a piece of the toast, and washed it all down with more coffee. He folded the paper and left it for the next patron.

The waitress put the check on the counter, "So, was that a good enough breakfast that you'll keep coming back?"

"Everything you said it was going to be," he said as he put two dollars on the counter.

With a smile, she slid a piece of paper across the counter. On it was written 'Marie WA5-9837.' "In case you ever want to, you know, talk."

North smiled, "Didn't you give me your number once before?"

"I did, but you didn't call, and this is a new number. I moved."

"Thanks, doll." He put the paper into his pocket and crushed the Stratosphere onto his mop of hair.

The waitress followed North to the door and whispered, "If you need to warm up later, you've got my number."

"I'll keep that in mind." He pushed the door open and stepped back into the weather. The sun, just rising, was a glowing orb barely visible through the clouds on the east side of town.

Tiffin was already at this desk when North walked into the squad room. "Morning, Brick," Tiffin said as he looked up from the files he was going through. "You anywhere on the murder in Tin City?"

North shook the snow off his hat before he put it on the coat tree, "Nope. You anywhere on the body they found at Cooper Wells?"

"Nope. Nothing to go on. The girl's been dead for years. Doc Howard said she was about fifteen when she died, but there's no way to tell the cause of death."

"Anything in missing persons?" North clicked the lid to his Zippo shut.

"There are quite a few teenaged girls who have had missing person reports filed on them, but they're all closed cases."

North took a deep draw on his cigarette, "Hard to believe that no one missed their kid."

"There are a lot of children who aren't cared for," Tiffin reached into his pocket for a cigarette of his own.

"Anything to go on?"

"Doc Howard said the girl had a gap between her front teeth."

"How's that helpful?"

Tiffin pointed at his teeth, "He says that it's hereditary. So, maybe we look for a Sand Rabbit with a gap between their teeth."

"So, you're going to wander around looking for gap-toothed people and ask if they're missing a daughter?"

"I thought I'd start with the high school. See if anyone there remembers a girl who went missing four or five years ago."

North nodded, "While you're doing that, I think I'll give Doc Howard a call and see if he's got any new information on Cudlip." North looked up at the clock, "Where's Uher? He keeping banker's hours?"

"Old Dan has gotten into the bad habit of being late."

"The chief can't be too happy about that."

"I'm not!" Pete Cummings said as he stepped out of the elevator. "I've about had it with Mr. Uher."

Tiffin looked at North, "His wife kicked him out. He's been sleeping on couches where he can find them."

The chief looked between the two detectives, "I'm done dealing with his personal life. Tiffin, you and North start working together again. I'll deal with Uher when he decides to grace us with his presence."

"Okay, boss," North began, "Where do you want us to start?"

Cummings pulled his pipe from his jacket pocket and began to push moist tobacco into it, "A few days before Christmas, and we've got the body of a girl no one remembers and a vagrant no one cares about. I'm more interested in the girl. Keep working that."

"Okay, chief," Tiffin gave a little salute.

"Before we go," Brick picked up the phone, "let me see if Doc Howard has anything on Cudlip." The operator picked up, "This is Detective North; get me the coroner's office."

"Detective, this is Ruth. I just wanted to let you know how sorry we all are about Sylvia."

North recalled the buxom redhead in the telephone exchange who had started shortly before he was suspended. "Thanks," it was the only thing he could think of to say. Moments later, he heard the telephone ring on the other end of the line.

"Doctor Howard."

"Doc, it's me, North."

"Brick! I was just finishing up on Cudlip."

"Find anything of use?" North lit a cigarette.

"Once I pulled his scalp back, I'm pretty confident the weapon was something with square edges."

"Like a two-by-four?" North pulled a piece of loose tobacco off his lip.

"No, this would have to be much harder than a two-by. Maybe a piece of angle-iron or a brick."

"Okay. So our victim was hit in the head by something square-edge and hard. Did he die instantly?"

"No. He died slowly. His crushed skull caused a brain bleed. He probably died over a couple of hours."

"That's got to be painful."

The doctor shook his head, "Thank God there are no pain receptors in the brain. But the skull fracture would have hurt like hell. We can only pray that he was unconscious from the blow."

"Okay, Doc, "North blew smoke toward the ceiling, "I'll look around for the murder weapon." North replaced the handset onto the cradle of the phone. "Doc says that something hard and square killed Cudlip."

"That's what I gathered." Tiffin pulled on his suit jacket and overcoat. "So, off to LaSalle High?"

North grabbed his jacket, "This snow is going to have covered up any clues that might be out at Tin City anyway, So off to the school."

Tiffin checked out the Ford Mainline from the motor pool. Both detectives were surprised that another couple of inches of snow had fallen. North slid into the passenger seat as Tiffin fired up the engine. "If the wind starts to blow, this snow is going to drift."

North nodded his agreement as he lit a cigarette, "Nothing like a good snow before Christmas to put everyone in the mood."

Tiffin could not tell if North's remark was sarcasm or not. He decided it must be. What should have been a five-minute drive to the school took nearly ten. The snow was being driven by winds off the lake; visibility was near zero at times. "I don't know, Tiff," North said as he blew smoke from his nose, "This doesn't look like it's going to let up."

"I think you're right. Let's get to the High School and then back to the office." They pulled up in front of the old red brick building. Students were pouring out of the doors, bracing themselves against the storm that nearly pushed the smaller children over.

North held his hat against the wind. Pushing past the children, they entered the warm halls of the school. "Where's the office?" North asked a student who was running by. The boy pointed behind him as he rushed to the door. A woman was just closing the door, "Excuse me, gentlemen. We're closing due to the storm."

Tiffin pulled his badge from his overcoat pocket, "I'm Detective Tiffin, and this is Detective North. We have just a couple of quick questions."

The woman looked aggravated, "I need to get home, too."

"This will just take one minute," North spoke calmly. "Were you working here five years ago?"

"Yes, I've been here over ten years now."

"We're trying to backtrack a student that may have gone missing. Female, five-foot-five, about fifteen, dark hair. She had a gap between her front teeth."

The office worker looked between the detectives, "We've got a lot of kids who come and go. I can't remember all of them."

North added some charm, "It would be very helpful if you could try to remember a young girl who may have just stopped showing up for class."

"I'm sorry, gentlemen, I just don't. Now, if you don't mind, I live out near Coloma. It's going to take forever to get home in this weather."

"Would you notice if a child didn't come back from summer vacation?" Tiffin asked, thinking about the sundress the body was found in.

"Look, Detectives, children come, and they go, especially during summer vacation." She shut the office door and slid her arms into her coat, "Now, if you don't mind. I don't want to get stuck and not get home." She brushed past the detectives and walked out of the building.

"She was friendly," North lit a cigarette as they walked out into the developing storm.

"Yeah, like a badger," Tiffin responded as he got the Ford started. The windshield wipers had trouble keeping up with the accumulation of snow. Back in the Safety Building, Tiffin stamped his feet on the mat, trying to get some of the snow off. "I think I'm going to head home before I can't get there. What say you?"

"Naw," North lit a cigarette. "I'm good for a while."

"Don't wait too long. Snow's apt to be worse down near the lake where you're living."

"Thanks, mother!" North turned and headed for the stairs. A voice called out from the telephone exchange, "Brick?" North stopped cold; for a moment, he forgot that Sylvia was gone. He took a deep breath and turned toward the voice. It was Ruth.

"Hey, you doing okay? Is there anything I can do for you?" Ruth's smile was stretched almost as tight as her sweater.

"I'm fine," North tried to sound like he was. "I don't think I need anything right now."

"I'm on until four if you change your mind."

"Ruth?" Midge, the switchboard manager, called out, "Is it time for your break?"

"No ma'am," Ruth rushed back into the telephone exchange and plugged her headphone back into her board, "LaSalle Harbor Police, how may I direct your call?"

In the squad room, North added to the case file of Jane Doe. He walked to the coffee urn and poured the few ounces of sludge he could manage to get out of the bottom. He added a few ounces of water from the cooler and looked out the window.

"Snows coming down pretty hard," it was Chief Cummings voice. "Why don't you think about going home?

"You're going to need a detective here to take any calls that come in." North lit a cigarette.

"No need to worry about that. I have it covered."

"How's that?" he took a deep pull on the Pall Mall.

"Uher is going to be on call at night for as far into the future as he could possibly imagine."

"Dan agreed to be on call permanently?"

"Mister Uher needs a place to sleep. We have a day room that's hardly ever used. He sleeps here in exchange for taking the calls that may come in." Cummings began to pack his pipe.

"And he's good with that arrangement?" North asked incredulously.

"No," Cumming chuckled. "But it was either that or be busted back to patrolman on graveyards."

"Ouch! That wasn't much of an option."

"The interim mayor is expecting me to run a tight ship. You could do well to remind yourself that the day starts at eight and not when you wake from a hangover."

30

"I don't suffer from hangovers, Chief," North protested.

"Well, you sure as hell don't seem to enjoy them!" The chief turned and walked into his office.

North spent a couple of hours pouring over case notes from the time that he was on leave. He made some mental notes on things to follow up on.

The chief came out of his office mid-afternoon, "Okay, North. The State Police have closed the highways, and a couple of bridges have been closed due to ice. We're shutting the building down."

"It's a little snow."

"No, it's a lot of snow. Shops are closed or are closing. It's time for you to go home for the day."

"So you're leaving this in the hands of Uher?" North shook his head.

"I wouldn't do that! The fire department is on their side of the building should Uher try to burn the place down. Now, get your butt out of here!"

North turned off his desk lamp before he grabbed his jacket and hat, "You're leaving, aren't you, chief?"

"I'm right on your heels. One phone call to make."

On the first floor, North headed for the back exit hoping he could tell his pickup from the myriad of cars in the lot. He had just passed the telephone switchboard when he heard his name. It was Ruth.

"Brick? Can you help a damsel in distress?"

North looked at the floor and shook his head, "Sure, doll. What do you need?"

"The buses have stopped running, and I live way out at Spink's Corners. Do you think you could give me a ride home?"

"I don't know, doll. That's a long way."

She gave a reserved grin, "Please, there's no one who can help."

"I thought you didn't get off work until four?"

Ruth turned to her supervisor, "Since I live so far out, she agreed to let me leave early."

"Get your stuff; the weather isn't going to wait for you." North knew he was going to regret this. He pushed the backdoor open against the snow that had drifted against it. "See that taller lump of snow?" he used his head to point toward a large pile of snow. "That's the chariot this damsel is taking home." They walked through the snow. North used his arm to brush snow off the passenger door, "Climb in."

He walked around to the driver's door and pulled it open. The Dodge fired up the first try. North brushed as much snow off the truck as he could before climbing back in. He let the pickup warm for a few minutes, "We better get going before I have to get the snow off this thing again." He slowly released the clutch and allowed the truck to roll forward. He got to the road and turned east. They had barely gotten two miles when the road became too snow-covered to continue.

"Come on, Ruth. There's got to be someone in town you can stay with."

"I don't know anyone. I'm pretty new here." She paused for a moment, "Maybe I can stay with you?"

North shook his head, "I just don't think that's a good idea."

"Look, I won't tell anyone. There won't be any gossip or anything."

"I could care less about gossip. I just prefer to be alone." North found a place he could make a three-point turn and headed back toward town.

Ruth was nearly in tears, "I'm sorry to ask this. But where am I supposed to stay?"

"Okay," he finally said, "But I do my thing, and you do the door mouse thing."

Ruth looked confused, "Door mouse thing?"

"Yes, as in quiet as…."

"Oh, a door mouse. Got it." She looked down, "Yes, absolutely."

North had his doubts.

The roads back to downtown were almost as bad as what they had just retreated from. The lightweight rear of the pickup fishtailed through snow-covered streets. North held his breath as he drove the curved road that led down to the lakefront. Against all odds, he managed to finally pull into the driveway. The pickup rode up a snowdrift and stopped. "Well, doll. This is it."

North opened the side door of the house and led Ruth into the kitchen. Gatto met them with a loud cry.

"Who's this," Ruth's voice took on a child-like affectation. "Oh, you are so cute," she rubbed Gatto's head. "I wouldn't have thought you'd own a cat."

"I don't own a cat," North said as he hung up his wet jacket and fedora.

"But he's here."

"He moved in with me."

"Oh, he came with the house when you bought it?"

"Yeah, something like that." He looked around the house, "Look, there's not a lot to eat, but you're welcome to what there is. I have a bad habit of sitting up half the night, so you take my bed, and I'll sleep on the sofa."

"I wouldn't think of taking your bed. The sofa is fine with me."

North shook his head, "Suit yourself."

Ruth looked through the kitchen and made supper, turning a few eggs, half a can of Spam, and some bread into a decent meal. After dinner, she listened to the radio while stroking Gatto. North sat on the sofa and sipped bourbon.

By ten o'clock, the wind had died down. North could not see out of the west-facing front door; the snow had drifted against the house's front. "I guess we better get you set up," He found a sheet and a heavy blanket. These, along with one of the pillows from North's bed, made a reasonable spot on the sofa for Ruth. North grabbed the bottle of Old Quaker and walked into the bedroom, "If the cat bothers you, kick him out."

"I couldn't kick him out in this weather."

"Suit yourself. Oh, there's a couple of clean towels in the closet in the bathroom." He shut the door to his bedroom, took off his clothes, and stretched out on the bed. As happened almost every night, the ghosts of the past came to haunt him. In his mind, he was back in the Ardenne, still separated from his unit and certainly behind enemy lines, "Fuck, the guys probably think I'm dead," He said to himself.

When darkness came, Sergeant North began walking west, hoping to catch up with an American unit. After he had walked for several hours, he had encountered neither friendly nor enemy troops. He sat, huddled under some brush when he heard a voice in the distance. He struggled to make out what it was saying. The sound seemed to come from every direction, "Brick? Where are you? I can't find you!"

It was Sylvia, but where was she? "I'm over here!" He stopped and listened. Only the sounds of the forest could be heard. "Where are you? Come here," he shouted.

The door to the bedroom squeaked open; Ruth poked her nose in, "Did you call me?"

North bolted upright, swung his feet to the floor, and sat shaking at the edge of the bed. He grabbed the bottle of whiskey and downed a couple of ounces.

"What?!" North realized he wasn't alone. For a moment, still, in the fog of his nightmare, he reached out his arms, "Sylvia!"

Ruth stepped into the bedroom, "Hey, you're okay."

North reached out and held her, but the shape was wrong. He shook his head, trying to release the fog, "Sylvia?"

"You've had a nightmare. It'll be okay."

He ran his fingers through his hair and shook. Ruth sat next to him on the edge of the bed and held him. After a while, they fell back onto the mattress, and she pulled the covers over them. She wrapped a leg over him and tried to still the shivering. "Shhh," she whispered, "whatever it is, it'll be okay."

North fell into a deep sleep, and eventually, Ruth also drifted off, warm against him. Before dawn, North woke. He was surprised to find the redhead in her underwear sleeping next to him. Surprised but agreeable. It had been months since he had felt a woman's touch. Her head was on his chest, and her breath was warm. He stroked her hair, she lifted her head, and they kissed. Their lovemaking was the frantic kind shared between two lonesome people.

Morning came late. The world was silent as it can only be when all the sound is absorbed by frigid air and a blanket of snow. Ruth stroked North's chest, waking him. "Hey, Brick," she whispered.

"Hey, Ruth." North stretched.

She pushed herself up on an elbow and looked at him, "What we did last night, did that mean anything?"

35

North shook his head, "What we did last night was the right thing at the moment. But," he paused, "I don't think that in the long run, it's the right thing for either of us. We're both lonely. That's all."

Ruth stood, picked up the shirt North had worn the day before, and covered herself, "I'm not as lonely as I was," she sighed.

He contemplated her words for a moment, "I'm not either."

"Do you have any coffee around here?" North nodded and walked her into the kitchen. Within a few minutes, the pot was perking on the stove.

"I don't suppose you have cream and sugar around here?" Ruth asked as he poured black liquid into a chipped cup for her.

"There's a bottle of milk in the fridge but no sugar."

North sat across the table from her and poured some bourbon into his coffee. "You drink a lot, don't you?" Her comment was not accusatory.

"I have a lot to forget," he said as he sipped from his cup.

Ruth looked at him, "You're not trying to forget last night, are you?"

"No," he thought about their lovemaking. "I want to remember that."

They sipped their coffee in silence for a while, "So, what's to eat around his place?" She stood and looked through the GE refrigerator.

"I've got some cereal, and there are eggs."

"We had eggs last night. I guess cereal will work."

North pulled a box of Corn Flakes from the cabinet. Ruth poured a bowl. "Don't you want some?"

North shook his head, "Just coffee." He took another sip, "what's today?"

"What's today?" Ruth seemed surprised by the question. "It's Saturday."

"Great, I'm not late." He paused, "Do you work today?"

"No, I'm not due until Monday at eight."

He looked out, "Good, it might take until then to dig out." She looked past him into the side yard. Snow had drifted well over the hood of the truck.

Ruth stood and walked over to North, the shirt hanging open, "So, what are we going to do this weekend?"

Chapter 4

Monday morning found North arriving at the office before eight. He and Ruth had eaten a hearty breakfast at the Howard Johnson's, somewhere he was sure they wouldn't be recognized. Tiffin arrived just after him, "You're early!"

North lit a cigarette, making a mental note that he was going to need another carton, "The chief said that this place was going to be run like the Marines, and he expected me on time."

Tiffin nodded and repeated a phrase he had heard too many times in the Navy, "Sweepers, Sweepers, man your brooms. Give the ship a clean sweep down both fore and aft! Sweep down all decks, ladders, and passageways! Dump all garbage clear of the fantail! Sweepers."

North laughed, "Yeah, at least I didn't have to sweep in the Army."

The red light on the coffee urn indicated the brew was complete. Both detectives grabbed a cup. "So," Tiffin said over the steaming cup of acidic liquid, "How long did it take you to dig out of your driveway?"

"I didn't."

"Your pickup is still at your place?"

38

"No, I didn't do the digging. A couple of kids with shovels came by and offered."

"How long did it take them?" Tiffin lit a smoke.

"I don't know, an hour and a half, two hours, maybe."

Tiffin shook his head, "Wow. What did they charge you?"

"Two dollars." North took another sip of the coffee.

"That's not bad bank for a couple of hours work."

North looked at his partner and smiled, "I gave them five."

Coffee almost came out of Tiffin's nose, "You gave five dollars for two hours work? Where do I sign up?"

"Come on, Tiff. The people down at the lake don't have deep pockets; I don't mind helping them out a bit." He lit a cigarette, "Besides, they'll be fighting over who keeps the snow clear and the lawn mowed."

Cummings stepped out of his office, "Get your hats and coats; I just got a call. They've found two more bodies down at Cooper Wells."

North picked up the phone and was immediately connected to one of the operators at the switchboard. It wasn't Ruth, "How may I help you, detective?"

"Detective Tiffin and I are heading over to the Cooper Wells building."

"Yes, sir," the line disconnected.

Bundled up against the cold, they got the Ford started and scraped the windows. It was close to twenty minutes before they finally arrived at the former hosiery factory. A worker in bib-overalls and a green steel hardhat flagged them down.

"You the police?" He asked.

North held the Stetson against the wind, "Yeah, I'm Detective North, that's Detective Tiffin. What have you got?"

"Come inside. I'll show you."

It was nearly as cold inside the abandoned factory as it was out. The only saving grace was there was no wind. North walked with notepad in hand, "Your name?"

"Mike Scherer."

North scratched a note, "And who do you work for, Mr. Scherer?"

"Merrick and Sons. They're in charge of the demolition on site."

"And your job?"

"I'm the site foreman."

North nodded as they walked into the bowels of the building, "Where did you find the bodies?"

"Well," the foreman stopped to consider his words, "they're not so much bodies as you know, bones. They're just around the back of that wall." Scherer pointed to a brick wall in front of them. As they approached the wall, they noticed several workmen talking and smoking, "You're not getting paid to stand there! Get back to work!"

"Yes, Mr. Scherer," one of the workers said. The group moved on. The detectives noted a large worktable had been moved away from the wall.

"They're behind the workbench," Scherer used his head to point. "The guys were pulling it out to get to the wall when they found them." On the ground were two sets of skeletal remains. Judging from the clothing, they were probably teenaged girls.

"These two make three that we've found in here," Scherer noted.

"We're aware," North examined the remains.

40

He had just begun to take a serious look when Doc Howard came up behind him, "If you're planning on doing my job, I can take the day off."

Tiffin lit a cigarette, "Nah, we'll let you do your work." He and North stepped aside. Doc Howard lowered himself down on one knee and examined the remains, "Judging from the lack of fusion of the pelvic girdle and the dentation, I'd say these remains are both girls in their early teens just like the other Jane Doe remains. I'll know more when I get them back to the morgue."

"I don't suppose there's any indication as to the cause of death," North said as he looked over the coroner's shoulder.

Howard carefully moved a skull aside. "Well, this one has a broken hyoid bone."

"How's that?" North asked.

"The hyoid bone is broken," the doctor repeated. Seeing a blank look on the detective's faces, he added, "It's a small bone under the jaw; some call it the tongue bone. It's nearly impossible to break by accident. I'd say this girl was deliberately choked to death."

North looked between the coroner and Tiffin, "So, three teenaged girls, murdered and dumped in an abandoned factory. Were they murdered here?"

Tiffin shrugged, "No way of knowing."

"Where are they from?" North thought aloud.

"Don't know."

"I'm in my eleventh year with the department," North paused to light a Pall Mall, "and I don't remember any string of missing girls."

"Maybe they were murdered elsewhere and brought here," Tiffin offered.

"Why would someone come here to dump a body, Tiff?"

A light seemed to come on behind Tiffin's eyes, "Maybe they were brought here and murdered."

"Exactly what I was thinking, partner. But from where?" North took a drag on his cigarette. He turned his attention to the coroner, "How long do you figure these girls have been dead?"

"This is purely speculation," The doctor paused and thought, "But three to five years. It's tough to tell."

"You said the first victim had been dead four to five years. Are you saying these bodies are newer than that?"

"I'm just guessing here, Brick."

"I know, Doc. But we've got bodies that could have been here from three to five years."

The doctor shook his head, "I'm not following."

"What if a girl was dumped here once a year for three years?"

The doctor looked at North and nodded, "I see what you're saying."

North studied the remains of the two victims, "Any way of telling what time of year they were dropped here?"

Howard shook his head.

"Any idea if these two were dropped together or separately?"

"Brick, I hate to tell you this, but there's just nothing to go on. I've got skeletons to work with. If I find anything other than the broken hyoid on the one victim, I'll let you know."

Tiffin made some sketches of the area where the bodies were found, while Doc Howard took a couple of polaroids.

"Mr. Scherer," North looked at the foreman, "I'm going to bring a few officers in to do a little more digging around."

"You know, I'm on kind of a tight schedule."

"Our guys poke around, or we shut you down. You're choice," North lit another cigarette and clicked the lid to his Zippo closed while he gave the foreman a moment to think.

"Fine. Guys are pretty much only thinking about the holiday break anyway."

The detectives added to the case file back at the Safety Building before wandering to the Trophy Room for lunch. "Hey Brick, Hey Tiff," Roxy called from behind the bar. Anything different than every time you're in here?"

North laughed, "Wouldn't want to throw you off your rhythm."

The waitress looked at Charlie, her husband, who was frying up a couple of burgers, "We're too old for the rhythm method anyway." She laughed at her joke while she got their order together. Placing two beers and a shot on the corner table the detectives occupied, Roxy whispered, "You know what they call women who use the rhythm method?" she looked at North and Tiffin, "Mom!" She laughed all the way back to the bar.

After lunch, they caught the chief up on their findings, "It's unacceptable!" Cummings clenched his pipe between his teeth. "There's got to be something to go on!"

Tiffin looked down; North looked his boss in the eye, "We've got some pieces of clothing and shoes. We have hair and teeth. But there's no way for us to identify who these girls are."

"Have you looked in the missing persons' files?"

"We've searched Michigan and have contacted the State Police in Indiana and Illinois. But, so far, we've come up empty-handed."

The chief looked at his detectives, "And I suppose Alvin Pates is still nowhere to be found."

"He's out there on the lam. We'll find him. He's just holed up someplace."

Cummings looked North in the eye, "And what are you doing to find him?"

"We're going to check every flop, boarding house, cheap hotel, and shelter in the area," North pressed the Stetson onto his head and looked at Tiffin, "Aren't we partner?"

By half-past four, the detectives had returned. Cummings was waiting for them, "Well?!"

"Chief, there's a lot of ground to cover…."

Cummings interrupted, "I'm not interested in Pates; I want to know about this." He held the afternoon edition of the LaSalle Palladium in front of them. Its banner headline read, "Sand Rabbit Murders." The subhead read, "Three Murders, Detectives Stumped."

The chief threw the paper onto the closest desk, "Which of you knuckleheads tossed a bone to a reporter?"

North got defensive, "You're joking, right? I don't talk to those hacks."

Cummings turned his gaze to Tiffin, who answered, "I'm with Brick. They can twist things around fast enough to make your head spin."

"Well, somehow they got a hold of this, and I want to know who decided to blab to the press," Cumming walked into his office and slammed the door hard enough the frosted glass in the window vibrated.

Tiffin and North looked at each other. "Uher," they said in unison. Not surprisingly, Dan Uher was nowhere to be seen.

44

By quarter past five, the sun had dipped into Lake Michigan. The sky was exceptionally clear; the new moon offered no competition for Orion, whose spear pointed toward the earth. The detectives had just completed their case notes when Tiffin stood and turned off his desk lamp.

"You planning to work a full day at some point?" North jested.

"Kaye and I are going to a Christmas party tonight. I need to get home and cleaned up," Tiffin pushed his arms into his overcoat.

"I hate to be the one who points this out," North adopted a serious tone, "but I thought you were Jewish."

Tiffin smiled. "There's a difference between Jewish and Jew-ish," he emphasized the 'ish.' "Besides, who doesn't like a good party?"

North raised his eyebrows and bobbed his head from side to side, "Me, for one."

"You're hopeless," Tiffin donned his hat. "Have a good night."

North sat at his desk long enough to smoke a cigarette before he, too, turned off his desk lamp. On the way to the parking lot exit, he looked into the switchboard and to the chair that Sylvia had occupied. He felt an emptiness that was beyond his ability to put words to. Midge, the switchboard supervisor, bumped into him as she walked out of the room. "Oh, I'm sorry," she said before she saw who it was she ran into to. "Hey, Brick," she put a hand on his arm. "How're you doing?"

"I'm okay," he pushed the Stratosphere onto his head.

"Liar," Midge whispered as she gave his arm a squeeze. "We're all missing her."

Once in the Dodge, North turned east on Main instead of toward his house. A few minutes later, he pulled into the lot behind the Sheffield Building where Sylvia had lived. He climbed the fire escape to the second floor. As always, the door to the corridor was unlocked. There was no light coming from the transom window over Sylvia's door. He reached onto the ledge of the transom; the key was no longer there. North stood in the hall for a couple of minutes, reliving the memory of the door opening and Sylvia standing there. Finally, he placed the palm of his hand on the door and held it for a moment before exiting the way he had entered.

He slowly drove down Main toward Water Street, which would take him down to the beach and his house. Christmas decorations hung from light poles, and shop windows displayed their wares along with holiday trim. North took very little interest in any of it. He stopped in front of the Cooper Wells building and thought about the three bodies that had been found. Whoever had dropped the bodies hadn't bothered to bury them. They had only been hidden.

"Why?" North asked aloud. Were they dumped in a hurry? Perhaps. Or, maybe the killer didn't care if they were found. He lit a cigarette and stared at the old red-brick factory as he smoked. While his mind ran through scenarios, trying to find one that made sense, a car pulled up behind him. The spotlight that swept past his rearview mirror caught his attention. He rolled down the window about the time an officer approached.

"Everything okay here, sir," the officer said as he got to the pickup. Seeing it was North, the officer put on a more conciliatory tone, "Oh, hey, Detective. I didn't know it was you."

North eyed the young, beefy officer, "Brodeur! How the hell are you?"

Brodeur smiled, "I'm doing okay. I've just got assigned this beat."

"Good for you. This ought to be reasonably quiet at this time of year."

The officer nodded. "So, you thinking about the bodies found here?"

"Yeah," North picked a piece of tobacco off his lip and rolled it between his fingers before flicking it out the window. "I'm waiting for the building to tell me something."

"So, you came down here to see if the building was going to talk?"

North shook his head, "No, I have to drive past it to get home."

"Where are you living?"

"Over on the seven hundred block of Lake."

Brodeur nodded, "I'll make sure to pay extra attention to your street."

North was ready to tell the officer to pay attention to all the streets on his beat but said instead, "Thanks, Will. I appreciate it."

"Merry Christmas, detective."

Things didn't seem very merry from North's perspective. Not knowing what to say, he rolled up the window and turned toward his house. Two blocks away, he rolled into this drive and was met by Gatto singing for his supper. "Well, you little beggar. I see you've returned." It wasn't until North went to open the door that he noticed a package wrapped in holiday paper.

Picking up the package, North followed Gatto into the kitchen. After hanging up his suit and feeding the noisy cat, he finally opened the box. It was full of sugar cookies and a note, "Thank you, Mr. North, for allowing my sons to shovel your drive. And thank you for your generosity. Your gift will not soon be forgotten. Respectfully, Mrs. Adele Wolfe."

North ate a cookie and washed it down with a shot of bourbon. He sat in the living room and thought about the blonde he had lost to something too small to fight.

Chapter 5

Tuesday morning dawned cold and clear. The unobstructed winds that blew over Lake Michigan whistled through the cracks in North's house. The barkcloth curtains in the front room rustled with every gust.

North had a quick breakfast at the Fifth Wheel before heading up to the Safety Building. "Detective?" a voice called out from the switchboard as he walked by. It was Ruth.

"Yes?" he looked at the redhead at the switchboard.

"You have a message to call Doctor Howard."

"Thank you," he paused, pretending to think, "Ruth."

She smiled and turned back to the board.

Upstairs, he hung his coat and hat and picked up the phone. Ruth answered, "How may I help you, detective?"

"Ring me Doc Howard's office."

"Yes, detective. I'll call you back when I have him."

North put the handset down on the cradle and grabbed a cup of coffee. The phone rang minutes later, "Detective North."

"Hold for Doctor Howard," there was an audible click telling the detective that the call was connected.

"Hey, Doc. You come up with something?"

North heard a cigarette lighter click shut, "Well, to be honest, not much. But I do have a little something you might follow up on."

"I'm all ears."

"The dress on one of the bodies had a label from the Petersen Harned Von Maur department store."

"Never heard of it," North scratched a note on the desk blotter.

"You probably haven't heard of it because it's in Davenport, Iowa."

The significance wasn't lost on North. "That would be like a body showing up in Iowa with clothes from Rimes department store here. No one drives two hundred and fifty miles for a dress."

The coroner took a pull on his cigarette and exhaled slowly, "There are probably dozens of reasons someone could be wearing clothes from an Iowa store. A gift or something picked up on a trip."

North pulled his notepad from his pocket, "Give me all the details you've got on our victim."

The doctor read from his notes, "She had long brunette hair. Stood about five-foot-five. I'm guessing her age to be approximately fifteen at the time of death. She'd had several cavities, all of them filled with amalgam. No signs of broken bones other than the hyoid. I'd say she was a healthy child."

"You figure she's been dead three to five years, correct?"

There was a pause, "That's pure speculation on my part. Don't hold me to it."

"Thanks, doc. At least it's something to follow up on."

North looked at his watch; it was a quarter of eight. "Not even seven in Davenport," he thought to himself.

By the time Tiffin arrived at eight, North was on his second cup of coffee. "Morning, partner. What if I told you that at least one of the girls we found was from Iowa?"

Tiffin hung his hat and jacket, "Iowa?"

"Davenport, actually," North took a sip of coffee, a self-satisfied look on his face.

"How did you deduce that piece of information, Sherlock?"

"Doc Howard called, said that one of the girls had on a dress with a label from a Davenport department store."

"So, now we check with the Davenport PD for missing teenaged girls."

"Exactly," North lit a cigarette.

Tiffin's phone rang, "Detective Tiffin." He made a couple of quick notes while he listened. "Okay. We'll be right down."

"What've you got?" North looked with curiosity toward his partner.

"Officers picked up Alvin Pates last night for drunk and disorderly. He's in holding."

North pushed his arms into his suit coat, "So, what are we waiting for?" He was heading down the terrazzo stairs before Tiffin had finished speaking.

"Lou!" North shouted for the officer guarding the holding cells, "Where's Pates?"

The older officer looked up from the crossword he was trying to solve, "Cell three."

"Go get him." North turned and opened the door to the small interrogation room outside the barred door that led to the four holding cells in the Safety Buildings basement. Tiffin came running in just a North flicked on the fluorescent light.

The officer led Pates in and handcuffed him to the table, "Call me when you're done with him." Lou shut the door on his way out.

"Alvin Pates?" North pronounced the last name like the word 'baits.'

Pates, a man in his late fifties, looked like the drifter he was, "It's said, Pat-tess."

North eyed him, "What's that?"

"My name is pronounced Pat-tess, not Paits."

"Alright, Mister Pates," North used the phonation as given him. "Do you know why you're here?"

"Sure, I stole a few bottles of wine from that winery and got drunk. But, I got to be honest with you. I don't remember much after the third bottle." Pates laughed, "Nah, that's a lie. I don't even remember drinking the third bottle."

The detectives waited while Pates chuckled to himself, "We don't care about a couple of stolen bottles of wine."

"Oh, good. Then you can let me go."

North took the chance to chuckle, "Pates, I'm arresting you on suspicion of murder."

"Murder! Who'd I murder?"

"Mack Cudlip."

"What? Mack's dead?" Pates seemed genuinely surprised.

"When's the last time you saw Mr. Cudlip?" Tiffin asked.

51

"I don't rightly know. Maybe a week or so." Pates seemed worried, "You ain't gonna pin this on me. I didn't do nothing."

North looked at the drifter, "I've never arrested anyone who admitted to murder. You're no different. Now tell me, where were you when you were last with Mr. Cudlip?"

"We was down at Tin City. I was packing my kit on account of getting some work down in New Carlisle." Pates watched as North shook a cigarette from the package, "You think I could bum one of them?"

North lit Pates' cigarette and let him take a deep drag on it before continuing, "Who did you work for down in Indiana?"

"I was at the farm of a man named Arndt. Don't rightly know his first name. He came up lookin' for some laborers to help tear down an old barn. Me and a couple of the guys climbed into the truck and went."

"And when did you get back?"

"Yesterday morning. Got dropped off down near the winery. That's when I decided to snatch me up a few bottles."

Tiffin looked at Pates, "Is there anybody who can vouch for you?"

Pates stirred, "Ain't nobody seen me take the wine."

"Not the wine. If I call down to New Carlisle and ask at the Arndt farm, will they tell me you were there?"

"Oh, heck yeah. Fetch me my wallet. They paid me fifty dollars for seven days' work. Got me enough to stay out at Tin City most the winter."

"Let me ask you this," North pulled a loose piece of tobacco off his lip, "who had it in for Cudlip?"

"Ha! Ol' Mack stepped on lots of toes. So, lots of people, I guess."

"Anyone in particular?" Tiffin took up the questioning.

"Well. Mack was into Machine Gun for a few dollars. Maybe he wanted his money back.

"Machine Gun?" North shook his head. "Who the hell is Machine Gun?"

"I don't rightly know his Christian name. Everyone calls him Machine Gun 'cause his name's Kelly."

"Lou!" North shouted. The officer opened the door. "Take Mr. Pates back to his cell."

"Wait! I didn't kill nobody. Ain't you gonna let me go?"

"There's still the matter of the stolen wine and your arrest for being drunk. You'll need to wait for the judge to decide when you're getting out."

After Pates was taken from the interrogation room, Tiffin looked at his partner, "Machine Gun Kelly? Really?! Well, the gangster by that moniker died in federal prison a few years back. So I'm guessing this isn't the same guy."

"You think?" North asked as they climbed back to their second-floor office.

Tiffin chuckled.

North sat down at his desk, "What are you laughing about?"

"Pates has been working at the Arndt farm, and that's what I'm getting Benjamin as one of his Christmas presents."

"I'm not even going to pretend I know what you're talking about."

"I'm giving my son an Ant Farm for Christmas."

North shook his head and began to add to the notes in the Cudlip file.

A little past nine, North lifted the receiver on his phone. The line was answered at the switchboard. It was Ruth, "How may I help you, detective?"

"I need to speak to someone in missing persons at the Davenport, Iowa Police Department."

"I'll ring you back when I've connected the call," the line went dead.

One cigarette and a cup of coffee later, the phone rang. "North," he answered.

"Hold for Sergeant Vogel," there were a couple of clicks as the call was connected.

"Vogel."

"Sergeant, this is Detective North of the LaSalle Harbor, Michigan PD. A body of a young female was found here that may have a connection to your part of the world."

"Okay, Detective, can you describe the girl?"

"Brunette, five-foot-five or so, maybe fifteen, sixteen years old."

"Slim build or heavy?"

"No build," North lit a Pall Mall and snapped the lighter shut.

There was a pause on the line, "What do you mean no build?"

"We have skeletal remains of a five, and a half-foot-tall brunette that our coroner thinks was about fifteen at the time of her death."

"How is it that you've tied those remains to Davenport?"

"One of the items of clothing had a label from," he paused to check his notes, "the Petersen Harned Von Maur store."

"Petersen's? Yeah, that's a local store.

54

"Let me ask you this, she's been dead for three or more years. Can you do some digging and let me know if anything pops?"

"Around fifteen, you say?" there was an edge to Vogel's voice.

"That's our coroner's guess."

"Let me get back to you."

North shrugged, "Okay. I'm Rick North"

"Okay, Rick. I'm Joe Vogel. I'll give you a shout back after I've pulled some files."

Tiffin looked expectantly across the desk, "He have anything?"

"Not that he mentioned. But, he did react when I told him the girl was about fifteen."

"Think that means something to him?"

"Yeah, but what?" North took a drag on the cigarette he was smoking. "What say we head over to Tin City and see what Fuchs can tell us about this Kelly."

The drive down to the migrant camp was uneventful. The snow along the shoulder of the road was no longer white. Instead, it was a slushy shade of grey. North directed Tiffin to park next to the building that housed the kitchen. Inside were a half dozen men gathered around an electric heater; its coils glowed bright red.

"Any of you seen Fuchs?" North asked as he entered the building.

"Nah," one of the men answered, "He ain't been around most of the day."

"Then maybe one of you can tell me where I can find a guy named Kelly."

An older man picked up the question, "Ain't seen Machine Gun for nigh unto a week. Maybe more."

North nodded, "So, maybe you haven't seen him since the night that Cudlip got murdered."

"Can't say."

"Can't, or won't? North fished the Pall Malls from his pocket and lit one.

The laborer looked between the two detectives, "What's the difference? I've said too much already."

"Well, is Kelly the last name or first name?" Tiffin asked.

"Don't know," the older man said, "and don't care. Just leave me alone." He turned back to the others at the table. It was evident that there wasn't going to be further conversation.

Chapter 6

There was a message waiting for North to contact Sergeant Vogel in Davenport. He took a moment to pour some coffee and light a cigarette before asking the switchboard to connect the call. Ruth answered the line.

"How may I help you, Detective?"

"Ring me back to the Davenport PD, Sergeant Vogel."

"I'll let you know when I have him."

He had hardly finished his cigarette when his phone rang, "North."

"Hold for the Davenport PD," there were a couple of clicks on the line before he heard Vogel's voice.

"I think I might have something for you."

North picked up his pencil, "Talk to me. What've you got?"

"I've got a couple of missing girls between fifteen and sixteen. Don't know which one you've got."

"You have a description?" North lit another Pall Mall and picked a piece of tobacco off his lip.

"Both are about five and a half feet, both brunette. One's been missing three years this June. The other is going to be five years ago, also in June."

"What else can you tell me?"

"The older of the two cases involves one Debra Haid. She was sixteen at the time of her disappearance. The other was Nancy Webber, fifteen."

North jotted in his notepad, "You seemed interested when I mentioned the remains I have were from a girl approximately fifteen years old. Why was that?"

"Probably just a weird coincidence, but both girls were part of the same girl scout troop."

"What's a scout troop, maybe a dozen kids?" North took a deep pull on his cigarette.

"There were ten girls in this troop, and over a couple of years, two of them disappeared."

North nodded, "One-in-five girls disappear from a group doesn't sound coincidental to me."

"There's another thing," Vogel added. "Their girl scout troop did this thing at Mercy Hospital where they learned about blood types."

"Go on," North prodded.

"Both girls had the same blood type; O-negative."

"That special, somehow?"

"I'm told that less than one in fifteen have that blood type."

North grew impatient, "Vogel, the question is, 'so what?'"

"Here's the thing. The doctor I spoke to said they call those with O-negative blood 'universal donors.'"

North's pencil hovered over his old leather notepad, "So, someone took them for their blood?" Tiffin looked up with a quizzical look on his face.

"I'm beyond speculating. But two girls from the same girl scout troop both have the same blood type and end up missing."

"That's no coincidence!" North crushed out his cigarette. "Any chance you have dental records for your missing girls?"

"I can get them to you in Thursday morning's mail."

"This is Tuesday." there was irritation in North's voice, "What's wrong with today?"

"I don't know about there in Michigan, but it's Christmas Eve in Iowa. I'm out of here at noon. I'll get those records in Thursday's mail." Vogel paused for a moment, "Merry Christmas." The line disconnected.

North replaced the headset on the cradle and looked at Tiffin, "So, two girls who were part of the same girl scout troop went missing two years apart, and they shared the same blood type."

"I wondered what you were talking about when you said they were taken for their blood."

"Why grab a girl in Iowa and bring her to Michigan?"

"Why grab a girl with a specific blood type and bring her to Michigan?"

North lit a cigarette and blew a smoke ring toward the ceiling lamp as he thought. He picked up the phone, "This is Detective North. Get me Doc Howard." He replaced the headset and continued to smoke.

"What are you thinking?" Tiffin asked as he got a cup of coffee from the urn in the corner.

"I want to know what reasons the doc might come up with for someone bringing a personal blood bank with them."

The phone rang, "Hold for Doctor Howard." The line clicked a couple of times indicated the call had been connected, "Doc, Brick North."

"Hey, Brick. What can I do for you?"

"Got a question. Why would someone want to kidnap a teenage girl with a specific blood type?"

The doctor mulled over the question for a moment, "Why do you think this has anything to do with a blood type?"

"Two girls matching the general description of the bodies we have went missing, and both had type O-negative blood."

"Universal donors," the doctor pondered aloud.

"So, why do I need to bring a universal donor with me from Iowa? Isn't there blood available here if I need it?"

"Yes, a doctor or hospital can secure blood when it's needed. It would be much more difficult for a private citizen to secure blood."

North, who had been leaning back in his chair, sat up, "How much more difficult?"

"Impossible, actually." The doctor paused for a moment, "I can't think of a single way someone could get blood."

"Okay. I can't go to the market and buy a quart of blood. But why would I need to?'

"Well, one could have cancer or anemia. Perhaps they have a bleeding disorder such as hemophilia," Howard lit a cigarette. "But, if any of those were the case, they'd be under a doctor's care."

"So, if I have O-negative blood, I can give it to anyone. Is that the case?"

"Yes, anyone can receive blood from someone with O-negative blood. The rub is that they can only receive from someone with the same blood type."

"So, this O-negative person gives to anyone but can only get it from someone with the same type. Got it."

"Does this have something to do with the remains I have down here?"

North took a drag on his cigarette, "It's possible that two of the girls had O-negative blood."

"I suppose I can try to extract marrow from the femurs of each girl and see if I can type the blood. But, I've got to tell you that after putrefaction, the odds get pretty damn slim."

"I've got dental records coming for two of the girls," North flipped his notepad closed. "I should get those end of this week, first of next."

Howard relaxed, "That'll be a far better way to ascertain identity. It'll be good to give these girls a name and get them back to their families."

"Okay, doc. Thanks for your help." North hung up before the coroner could respond.

North and Tiffin spent the rest of the morning tracking down known felons named Kelly. Tiffin looked up with exacerbation from the stack of three-by-five cards on his desk, "I didn't realize that so many people called Kelly have ended up in the Michigan Department of Corrections."

"Let's narrow it down." North looked up from his own stack, "How many Mr. Kelly's have a connection to Douglas County?" The two detectives began sorting cards. Within a few minutes, they had narrowed their list to less than thirty possibilities. Around noon, North stood and grabbed his hat and coat, "Let's grab some lunch."

Tiffin followed North down the stairs.

The Trophy Room was busier than usual. Office workers and some shopkeepers were packed into the ordinarily quiet bar. A scantily clad blonde in a white fur-trimmed red velvet vest, matching panties, and heels danced through the bar holding a sprig of mistletoe over her head. North caught Roxy's attention, "What's this?"

"Meet 'Miss Santa Claus.'"

"Charlie's idea?" North shouted over the noise.

Roxy nodded as she shook her head, "Yeah, but you gotta admit it's brought some traffic in."

As the detectives found a table in the back of the bar, the blonde danced their way and plopped down on North's lap, "Hey, Brick. Long time no." She wrapped her arms around his neck and planted a kiss on his forehead.

"Tiff, you recognize Renee Vivienne, don't you?"

Tiffin nodded, "Renee, I haven't seen you since I was working vice."

She smiled, "Hello, Detective. I'm flattered you remember me." Then to North, "I haven't seen you since that night at the Swanson last summer."

Tiffin cocked his head, "Care to explain that, partner?"

North chuckled, "Renee was trying to drum up some business one night in the lobby of the Swanson Hotel. I recommended she leave before she spent the night as a guest at the Safety Building."

Renee planted a kiss on North's mouth as she stood, "He's such a gentleman."

Roxy brought two beers and a shot of whiskey to the table, "So, you boys have plans for Christmas?"

"Chinese food and a movie for my family," Tiffin sipped his beer.

"How about you, Brick?"

North shook his head, "Forced day off for me. I'll probably just come here for lunch."

The big gal put her hands on her hips, "You won't be coming here; we'll be closed. But, you're welcome to join Charlie and me for Christmas dinner. There'll just be the two of us."

North downed the shot of whiskey and handed the empty glass back to Roxy. "Thanks for the invite, but I'll pass."

"Well, if you change your mind, you know where we live."

After the waitress had left the table, North looked at his partner. "I'm not much of a holiday person, but what's with Chinese food and a movie on Christmas."

Tiffin smiled, "It's kind of a holiday tradition my parents started. The only things open on Christmas Day in LaSalle Harbor are Hung Fong's Chinese restaurant and the Liberty Theater."

North took a sip of his beer, "You and Kaye really know how to live it up."

"Well, we all can't be as apathetic as you."

A beer bottle narrowly missed North's head before crashing into the wall behind him. Two well-lubricated patrons were fighting over who's lap Miss Santa was going to sit on next. Most of the other customers were content to ignore the whole thing. A few others apparently decided a bar fight was what was needed on Christmas Eve. Either way, the two detectives stepped into the middle of the action and broke up the dust-up. Over the protests of both men that they weren't drunk and really hadn't meant to start a fight, they were both thrown out of the Trophy Room.

Miss Santa, who had been knocked down during the brawl, sat on the floor trying to hold her vest together. Roxy stared at her husband and shook her head. Charlie tried to ignore his wife's glower. Tiffin and

North looked around the bar. "Anyone want to spend Christmas Day in jail?"

The excitement over, North helped Renee to her feet. Holding the vest, she exited into the backroom of the bar. "Okay, guys. The show's over," Charlie barked from behind the bar.

North grabbed the Stetson and held it out. "Alright. Now that the party has been ruined, let's see you throw some cash in here to pay for the," he paused to find the right word, "performer." He walked the hat to each person. With the hat full of cash, he strolled into the backroom where Renee was putting on her street clothes. "Here's a little something from your audience."

Renee smiled, "Most of this town wishes I'd just disappear. But you've always been nice to me." She gave him a little hug, collected the cash, and exited the back door into the alley.

Back in the bar, North had just sat down as Roxy put a burger in front of Tiffin and another shot of whiskey in front of him. He sipped the whiskey as Tiffin devoured the hamburger. "You hungry there, partner?"

"Kaye was sick this morning and didn't feel up to making breakfast."

"What about your kids? You leave them hungry, did you?"

"They're at Kaye's parents for a couple of days. They can celebrate the last night of Hanukkah with their grandparents."

North finished the whiskey, "How's that?"

"Think of it like Christmas for Jewish kids. But instead of being one night, it's eight nights long."

Not knowing what to say, North finished his beer in silence. "Okay. I'm heading back to the office."

"I'm going to run into Woolworth's. Need to pick up another gift for Kaye."

"Pressure cooker or vacuum cleaner for the missus this year?"

Tiffin shook his head, "If you must know, I'm going to get her some cologne."

North laughed, "Go get 'em, tiger!" The detectives settled up with Roxy, who gave them both a hug and a kiss on the cheek. Back at his desk in the Safety Building, North continued to flip through the three-by-five cards trying to lower the number of Kelly's they were going to have to interview. There were only three that were shown as 'transient.' He was both pleased and frustrated. Going from thirty to three was a huge step; trying to find transients felt like a step in the wrong direction.

When Tiffin returned, they created bulletins to distribute to the patrol officers to look for men who matched the descriptions of the three Kelly's. They worked with the desk sergeant on duty and his replacement to ensure that the bulletins would be distributed to as many officers as possible. It was almost three o'clock when they got back to the squad room. Chief Cummings was there with a bottle of scotch and several glasses.

"Who's going to join me in a toast?" he held a glass aloft. The detectives shared a toast with their boss. "It's good to have you back, North," Cummings said as he lit his pipe. "Good to have the team together."

Tiffin elbowed North and whispered, "You've got him in a sentimental mood. Now's the time to ask for a raise."

"Something tells me that it's the scotch that's got him in a sentimental mood."

"Drink up, lads!" Cummings held the bottle up.

"I need to head home to my wife," Tiffin grabbed for his coat and hat.

"How about you, Brick?"

North held his glass out for a refill, "I really don't know how you drink this stuff," he downed the amber liquid, "tastes like sweaty socks to me."

Cummings laughed, "That's because you drink whiskey from burned barrels." He held up his glass, "Scotch is the drink of peasants and kings, of laborers and poets, of lonely men and lovers. Now, why are you standing here? Get yourself home. I don't want to see your puss until day after tomorrow."

"You're the boss." North grabbed the Stetson and his coat and headed for the stairs.

A slightly inebriated chief called after him, "I'm sorry you can't be spending the holiday with Miss Kingston."

North crushed the fedora onto his head and pretended he hadn't heard anything. He automatically looked into the switchboard as he passed. It was an empty feeling he felt looking at someone else seated at Sylvia's station. "Merry Christmas, Detective," the switchboard supervisor called out."

"Merry Christmas, Midge," he responded as he avoided eye contact with any of the operators who were working. Once out the backdoor and into the Dodge, he smoked a cigarette while the flathead engine warmed up. Down on the lakefront, he parked in front of Damaske's Market at the corner of Park and Pine. He picked up a handbasket and grabbed a couple of potatoes and some eggs as he made his way to the meat counter. He looked over the handful of steaks lined up in rows separated by kale as two men spoke with each other behind the counter.

"A whole hank of casings? Is it the same guy who used to come by in the summer?"

"Yup. Same guy."

"Did you ask what he needs a hank for?"

"Nope. He seemed anxious and was willing to pay what I asked." The butcher looked at North, "What'll it be?"

"Fix me up with two of the best steaks you've got." North's curiosity got the better of him, "What's a hank of casings?"

"A hank," the older of the two butchers explained, "is one hundred yards of pig gut sausage casing."

"And someone came in and bought a hundred yards of casing. Not sausage, but just casing?"

"Yeah. He would come in once a week during the summer three or four years ago. Always the same thing, a hank of casings. Got to the point we had to order extra just to keep up with what he wanted."

North pulled back his jacket to reveal his badge, "I'm curious. What would someone need three hundred feet of sausage casing for?"

The butcher shook his head, "Unless he's making sausage, there's nothing that I can think of."

Grabbing his notepad, North started writing, "Can you describe this man?"

"Oh, average height; you know, five-nine or so. Probably fifty. He's greying at the temples. Kind of lean."

"How was he dressed?"

The butcher looked quizzically at North, "You know something hinky about this?"

"Don't know anything about it. But it's just peculiar enough to make me want to look into it. So, how was he dressed?"

"A bit better than most our customers. Nice blue wool winter jacket and a brown hat. Nice brown leather gloves, too."

"I don't suppose he wrote a check to pay for those casings?"

"Nope. He peeled off a twenty and handed it to me without so much as a question. Imagine paying the same as a week's worth of groceries for a small box of casings. Makes no sense."

"And that's it. That's all he bought?"

"Yup, came in, walked right up to the counter, asked for a box of casings, dropped a twenty of the counter, and left."

North scratched a few notes, "You didn't happen to see what he was driving?"

"Nope. Can't see much from back here. You might ask Janet up at the front." The butcher wrapped the two pieces of meat in white paper and used a wax pen to write the price on the package, "What else for you?"

Brick grabbed a couple of cans of pork and beans and some corn flakes on the way to the front. He put the basket on the counter next to the large brass cash register. "Will that be all, doll?" The cashier asked as she looked lustfully at North.

"No, the butchers were talking about a man who bought some casings. He was wearing a blue wool jacket and a brown hat. Did you happen to see what he was driving?"

"Uh, black or maybe blue, Oldsmobile. Or was it was a Buick?" She shrugged, "They all look the same. Maybe it was a Chevy."

The cashier rang up the two steaks, two potatoes, eggs, corn flakes, and pork and beans, "That'll be two forty-seven."

The sausage casing remained on North's mind as he sipped Old Quaker late into the evening. Finally, he fell asleep on the sofa, awakening only when the bells at Trinity Lutheran Church began tolling for the midnight service Christmas morning.

Once again, he was in the small village church in Freyneux, France. It was Christmas morning, 1944. Separated from his unit, he and another soldier had taken refuge in the ancient Chapelle du maître. The German's had broken the line and were taking the village, heading ever closer to the church. Bullets smashed through the centuries-old stained-glass windows as shoulders pushed against the massive oak doors that he had barred from the inside. A German "potato masher" hand grenade crashed through a window and landed with a thud on the flagstone floor just as the other soldier became Sylvia. Suddenly, he was watching the scene from outside the church. The grenade exploded, and he watched helplessly as shrapnel tore through her. Instead of falling, she remained standing, bleeding from hundreds of wounds. "Brick, where are you?" she screamed.

He awoke, shouting, "I'm here!" Shaking, he reached for the bourbon and took a mouthful. He held it in his mouth before allowing it to slowly slip down his throat.

North looked out the kitchen window to the thermometer nailed to the frame. It was thirty-one degrees. He donned the old Mackinaw and his hat and, along with Gatto, began his nightly walk. It was close to three before he finally crawled into bed. He was grateful to be exhausted enough that sleep came without a fight.

Chapter 7

A knock on the front door woke North from perhaps the best sleep he'd had in several weeks. It took him a moment to orient himself and pull some pants over his boxers. He grabbed the .38 from its holster, flipped it open, spun the cylinder, and clicked it closed.

North crossed the living room and looked out the curtain covering the oval leaded glass window in the door. A young woman in a cloth coat with a scarf tied over her hair stood outside with the two boys who had shoveled his drive a few days back. He pushed the gun into his pocket and opened the door, "Yes?"

The boys held a box which they pushed toward North. The woman spoke with a German accent. "We are sorry to have bothered you. I am Adele Wolfe. I am certain my sons you recognize. They wanted to wish you a Merry Christmas by bringing you *Lebkuchen*, a special Christmas cookie. We are sorry that we seem to have awakened you."

Looking down at his bare feet, wrinkled pants, and undershirt, North chuckled, "I had a long night and didn't get to bed until late."

"We will not bother you further. A good Christmas to you. Come boys, wish Mr. North a good holiday." The boys offered self-conscious wishes.

"*Frohe Weihnachten,*" North said as the trio was turning.

Surprised, Mrs. Wolfe turned back and looked at North, *"Du sprichst Deutsch?"*

North smiled, *"Nur ein bisschen."*

"Oh, it sounds like you speak more than a little. Your German is *sehr gut.*"

"Thank your husband for letting your boys bring the cookies."

Mrs. Wolfe looked down, "Mr. Wolfe was lost when the Steinbrenner went down in fifty-three." The SS Henry Steinbrenner was a Great Lakes Freighter that went down in Lake Superior during a storm in May of that year. Seventeen of the twenty-nine on board were lost.

"I'm terribly sorry," North hoped his words didn't sound hollow.

"It is okay; we have gotten used to our loss." She looked past North into the living room, "Forgive my rudeness, but do you not have a Mrs. North?"

North felt a hot lump in the back of his throat, "The woman I wanted to marry died a few months ago."

Mrs. Wolfe looked remorseful, "Oh, we have both brought up the *schlechte Erinnerungen*, the bad memories. Forgive me, please." She put her arms over the shoulders of her sons and led them off the porch.

"Thank you for the cookies," North called after them. He was confident that under the coat and scarf was an attractive woman who might be just as lonely as he was.

Gatto pushed his way through the open door and jumped onto the overstuffed chair. North gave the marmalade cat a scratch behind the ears as he walked into the kitchen to get the coffee going. He caught a glimpse of the clock on the stove as he put the percolator on the gas; nine-fifteen.

After a pot of coffee and a shower, North leafed through his case notes. About the time he was thinking of getting out of the house, there

71

was a knock on the front door. "Grand Central Station!" he called out as he grabbed the .38 from the kitchen table. A quick look out the window revealed Barry and Kaye Tiffin; Barry had several brown paper bags. North shrugged and opened the door.

"Brick!" Kaye exclaimed as she hugged him. "Oh, it's so good to see you!" She reached up and gave him a kiss on the cheek.

North looked toward his partner, "Which one of you decided I needed company?"

Tiffin gave a sideways glance toward his wife, "It was our idea." The emphasis was on the word, 'our.'

"And who did you bribe to find me?"

"You might not believe this, but I am a detective. You told me that you purchased a house on the seven hundred block of Vine. Short block, and only one green pickup to be found."

"And if the pickup and I had been gone, then what?"

"Then all of Kaye's cooking would be enjoyed back in our house instead of yours."

North chuckled, "So, what have you brought me?"

Kaye led the men into the kitchen, where she had her husband put the bags on the counter, "We've brought braised brisket with carrots, parsnips, and rutabagas. Latkes with sour cream and applesauce, and for dessert, *sufganiot*!"

North looked at his partner with a blank look on his face.

"Jelly doughnuts," Tiffin whispered.

"The brisket is cooked; it just needs to be warmed up in the oven. The latkes are ready; I just need to fry them. Tell me that you have a skillet and shortening."

"I've got a skillet and bacon drippings if that will work."

The Tiffins looked at each other for a moment. Kaye finally laughed, "Well, it's not like we keep a kosher home." She cooked while Barry pulled a bottle of Manischewitz out of one of the bags. North rinsed out a couple of coffee cups and handed one to Tiffin.

"You don't want any wine?" Tiffin asked as he poured a liberal amount of the sweet-smelling wine into the cup.

"Nah, I'm good," North poured a liberal amount of bourbon into the other cup.

Tiffin raised his cup in a toast, "To absent friends."

"To absent friends," North repeated. He downed the bourbon and poured another.

Kaye took it as an opportunity to talk, "So, how are you doing?" North began to say something as she put her hand on his shoulder, "And don't say that you're okay because you're not."

North lowered his cup to the table and stared out the window for a moment, "Honestly, I don't know. Angry? Empty? Sad?" He paused and sipped the bourbon before he finally spoke, "It's like an earthquake has rattled me from the floor to the top of my head." He put a hand on his chest, "My heart hurts. Does any of that make sense?"

Kaye dropped down to one knee and put her arms around him, "It makes perfect sense. In Yiddish, we say *troyer*, which translates as grief. But it means so much more." She thought for a moment, "Remorse, regret, anguish, sadness."

Tiffin sipped the wine, "It's not an earthquake you're feeling; it's a griefquake." His wife batted at him. He laughed, as did North, who shook his head.

"So, how'd you find this house?" Kaye asked as she returned to the latkes frying on the stove.

"I made a couple of calls, and this one seemed to have everything I needed," North took another sip of the bourbon.

"How many houses did you look at?" Kaye asked as she flipped a potato pancake.

"Just this one."

She looked at him in disbelief, "You bought the first house you looked at?

"How many did I need to see? This is fine." North nodded toward a narrow stairway in the corner of the kitchen, "It even has an attic that I could turn into a room for your husband if you ever kick him out."

Kaye went back to frying the latke, "Men!" she muttered under her breath.

During dinner, North outlined the conversation he had at the market. "Why would someone buy three hundred feet of sausage casing?" Tiffin asked with a mouthful of brisket.

"I'm probably spending too much time thinking about it, but it's eating at me. What exactly do you do with sausage casing without making sausage."

"What exactly is this stuff made out of?" Kaye asked.

Tiffin shook his head, but North answered anyway, "It's the lining of pigs' intestines."

Kaye put her fork down, "Ew. That'll teach me to ask."

"And," North pushed a forkful of brisket into his mouth, "the butcher said that this guy bought a lot of it during the summer months three or four years ago."

"That can't be a coincidence," Tiffin wiped his mouth. "We've got girls who died three or four years ago in the summer."

"So, let's put this together," North paused to think. "We have the remains of three girls. Two girls go missing from Davenport, Iowa. Both belonged to the same Scout troop. Both had O-negative blood. And some guy in LaSalle Harbor is buying sausage casing by the bushel."

"Well, since you put it that way…." Tiffin began.

"We've got nothing, " North replied.

Kaye waited for the men to stop talking, "Maybe he used the pig guts to tie the girls up. It would have rotted away just like their own skin did."

"Okay, that makes as much sense as anything I've thought up, but why buy more now?" North stopped and looked at Tiffin, "Unless he's got another girl here."

"Why would he take a girl from Iowa and bring her here to kill?" Kaye looked between her husband and North. "I mean, there are girls here, too."

"Well, if you kidnapped a girl in Iowa, no one would be looking for her here," North ran a piece of latke through the sour cream on his plate.

Tiffin shook his head, "Maybe this time the coincidence is just a coincidence."

North shook his head, "Nope. There's no such thing as a coincidence…."

"…only a connection we haven't made," Tiffin finished. "So, what's the next step?"

"Tomorrow morning, we call Vogel in Davenport and see if he's got any new missing person cases involving teenaged girls."

"With type O blood."

North speared the last piece of brisket on his plate. "With type O blood," he repeated.

After dinner and the jelly doughnuts and coffee, the Tiffins left to pick up their children. North sat, enjoying the quiet. Eventually, he got up and looked at the thermometer; it was nearly fifty degrees outside. Donning the Mac and his Stetson, he began to walk.

He climbed the seventy-three steps up to the bluff and walked toward Main. Ten minutes later, he found himself walking along Colfax Avenue. He recalled the heavy-breasted woman who had kissed ice cream from his lips last summer and smiled to himself. For just a moment, he considered knocking on Suzette's door but thought better of it.

His steps became a mantra that blocked any thoughts that might have crossed his mind. Time passed. As he walked back down Main, he was struck by the silence of the day. There was no traffic. The shops were all closed, as was every eatery except for Hung Fong's. The red neon "Chop Suey" sign glowed against the black glass front of the restaurant. The three round windows on the front of the restaurant revealed a few diners and what appeared to be the family enjoying their meal in the dining room's rear. As the sun sank into Lake Michigan, North was met by a hungry cat at the side door, "There you are, you little beggar."

Gatto danced between North's feet as the ration of Puss n' Boots was served. For himself, North finished the bottle of Old Quaker and fell into a drunken sleep on the sofa.

Chapter 8

Much of the workforce of LaSalle Harbor seemed to have taken the day after Christmas off. Shopkeepers were busy preparing their stores for business, but offices remained locked and dark. North dropped off his cleaning at Aristo Cleaners on Pipestone before heading to the Fifth Wheel for breakfast.

Marie poured a cup of coffee and put it in front of North, "What'll it be?"

He took a swig of the coffee, "For some reason, I've got sausage going through my head."

"Link or patty?"

"Link. Get me some fried potatoes, a couple of eggs over hard, and toast no butter."

Marie called back through the service window, "Couple of zeppelins, Pittsburgh some Murphy's, flop two over hard, dough no cow paste."

North looked at her, "Some of your lingo seems to have changed."

"New cook, so gotta learn new lingo." she looked around to make certain no one was within earshot and lowered her voice anyway, "I bet you could teach me a few things."

"You just might be right. But I'm not taking on any new students at the moment." Smiling to himself, North turned to the newspaper. Marie went to take an order at a nearby table; looking at North instead of where she was going, she ran into a chair.

A name on the front page of the Palladium caught his eye. "Brodeur," he said under his breath. "What has Will been up to?"

Frustrated Fugitive is All Shook Up

Michael Parsons, 41, of 293 Burton street, who allegedly was threatening two women with a butcher knife on Christmas Eve, found an attempt to escape from police a tough obstacle course. Officers Wilbur Brodeur and Larry Rogers rushed to 404 Paw Paw avenue at 11:14 p.m. Tuesday in response to a call that Parsons had Louise and Nancy Edwards cornered in a bathroom with a butcher knife. As the officers arrived, Parsons bolted upstairs and jumped off a back stairway onto the roof of a small storage shed. He crashed through the roof and went through the wooden floor inside. Struggling free, Parsons plowed into a tangle of loose wire in the backyard and fell. Righting himself, the would-be fugitive tripped into a hole that had been dug by the homeowner. After climbing out, he piled up against a fence that got in his way. The officers collared him against the fence. Parsons has been charged with drunk and disorderly. Other charges will follow.

North was still chuckling when Marie laid breakfast on the counter, "What's so funny?" she asked.

"One of my friends had to watch a criminal try to get away."

"Watch him try?" Marie refilled his coffee cup.

"I guess the guy wasn't very good at escaping."

After having inhaled his breakfast, North walked across the street to the Safety Building. Upstairs in the detective squad room, he found the coffee urn off and empty. He carried it to the slop sink in the janitor's closet and filled it with water. Inserting the stem and basket, he filled it with what appeared to be an ample amount of Folgers, replaced the lid, and plugged it in. The urn was just beginning to perc when Tiffin walked in, "You made coffee?"

"Why would I do that?" North smirked.

Tiffin hung up his hat and coat, he kept his suit jacket on, "Kaye wanted me to tell you that we had a good time at your house yesterday."

North lit a cigarette and plucked a loose piece of tobacco off his lip, "Oh, she did, did she? Did she want you to tell me anything else?"

"No," Tiffin looked at the coffee urn wishing it to complete its brew. "But she did tell me that you'd done alright on the house."

"She's just jealous that I bought mine, having looked at only one, and she probably looked at twenty before deciding on the one you have."

"Double that number, and you'd be closer."

About that time, Chief Cummings stepped off the elevator, "Good morning, boys. Where are you on any of your investigations?"

The detectives looked at each other for a moment before North spoke up, "Got an area broadcast out on the three transient Kelly's. I haven't checked yet this morning to see if officers have turned anything up. And, we're waiting for Davenport to get back to us with dental records of their missing girls."

"Okay," Cummings pulled his pipe from his breast pocket and began loading it with moist tobacco. "Anything else?"

North decided not to tell him anything about sausage casings, "No, that's it at the moment."

79

Cumming sucked flame into the bowl of tobacco, "I don't want to see you louts sitting around waiting for something to fall from heaven."

"No, sir," Tiffin began to pour a cup of coffee from the urn.

"How about you, North?" Cummings spoke through a cloud of smoke.

"I'm going to head down to Tin City and see if I can get any more on the Kelly character."

"When you hear from Davenport, let me know. I've got a reporter from the Palladium who is hounding me for information."

North took a drag on his cigarette, "Try to get them to stop with the Sand Rabbit thing. There's no evidence that these girls were local."

"And they'll argue that there's no evidence that they're not. Remember, reporters don't want facts; they want stories."

Cummings retreated to his office while North and Tiffin read through the blotters for Christmas Eve and Day. "Looks like one of our local boys was released from jail on Tuesday and attempted to rape a young woman on Christmas morning," Tiffin offered.

"Did they catch him?" North asked, not really looking for an answer.

"Yeah, he was found at the Shangra-La after starting a knife fight with another customer. Seems like the bartender used a pool cue to knock him out."

North acknowledged Tiffin with an "Uh-huh" while rereading an item on Christmas' blotter, "Someone tried to rob a cab yesterday at about 1:40 in the morning."

Tiffin looked up, "Nothing uncommon about that."

"Davidson collared him with the nine dollars he had taken still in his pocket."

Tiffin grew impatient, "Why is this important?"

"Because the guy Davidson collared is named Kelly," North crushed out the cigarette he had been smoking, "Kelly Edward George."

"You thinking…"

North cut him off, "That Kelly isn't Machine Gun's last name."

The two detectives raced to the holding cells on the basement level. "Lou! Which cell is Kelly George in?" North shouted as he came down the last flight of stairs."

"Four," Lou said as he put the pencil down on the crossword he was working on.

Picking up the keyring from the hook on the corner of Lou's desk, North unlocked the barred door that led to the corridor of holding cells. He swung the door open and called, "Machine Gun!"

"Who's asking?"

"I've got a couple of questions for you," North walked down the corridor, Lou right behind him. "Handcuff my friend here and bring him to the interrogation room," North unlocked cell number four.

Kelly's handcuffs were locked to the ring on the interrogation table. North gave him the once over. "Five nine, buck forty, middle-aged and balding. I thought someone calling himself Machine Gun Kelly was going to be a tough guy."

"Unchain me, and you'll see how tough I am."

North dismissively shook his head, "Hell, I take shits bigger than you, George."

"Let me loose, and we'll see who shits," George rattled the handcuffs against the table ring.

Tiffin slapped him on the back of his head, "Shut up."

"What the hell. I robbed a cabbie. I won't spend a month in jail, and in the meantime, I get room and board courtesy of the nice folks here in LaSalle Harbor. Don't sound too bad to me."

"Robbing a cab is the least of your worries," North lit a cigarette. "We want to talk to you about the murder of Byron Cudlip."

George attempted to stand, partially lifting the heavy metal table, "You can't pin that on me."

"You don't seem surprised that Cudlip is dead," Tiffin said from behind him.

"Hell, everybody's gonna die. Just a matter of when." the prisoner answered with a snarky tone in his voice.

"We understand that you had a beef with Cudlip," North lit a Pall Mall and blew smoke toward the flickering fluorescent lamp on the ceiling.

"So, I had a beef with him. He owes me three dollars; why would I kill him? Ain't never gonna see my money if he's dead."

"You loaned a floater with no way of paying you back three dollars, and you're upset he hasn't paid you. You're not as smart as you think you are," North took a drag on the cigarette.

"I loaned Mack two dollars. He owes me three. Interest and all. Pretty smart if you ask me."

North looked at his partner, "Old Machine Gun here is a wannabe loan shark."

"Ain't no crime trying to make a buck."

"Here's what I think happened." North took a drag on the cigarette, "You got yourself hurting for money, found Cudlip who couldn't pay up, and hit him over the head to show him you meant business."

Tiffin nodded, "Yeah, you didn't mean to kill him. It was just an accident."

George looked at North, "You got nothing on me except for me robbing some cabbie. You can't pin Cudlip on me."

"I go back to the fact that you're hurting for money, and Cudlip couldn't give you what he owed. That sounds like a motive to me. What about you, Tiff?"

Tiffin nodded, "Sounds like a reasonable motive to me."

"You're already under arrest for robbing the cabbie. I'm holding you on suspicion of the murder of Byron Cudlip."

"You can do what you want. I didn't kill Cudlip. The more you try to make stick, the more time I'm all warm and fed."

"It's a shame there's no death penalty in Michigan because I'd drive to Jackson to watch," North crushed out his cigarette. "We're done here." He looked toward the door, "Lou, come take Machine Gun here back to his cell."

Once the detectives were alone, Tiffin spoke up, "We've got nothing on Mr. George to hold him for murder."

"Maybe not yet. But the day's young. What say we call Vogel in Davenport and see if he's missing any more girls."

Thankfully, the call to Davenport did not uncover any new missing girls. After explaining that there were no new cases, Vogel went on, "You guys got me thinking. So, I made a couple of calls. Turns out that there's a teenage girl who went missing from Eldridge, which is a few miles up the road, about four years ago."

North took a sip from his cup of coffee, "So, what's the connection?"

"She was also a girl scout whose troop went to Mercy Hospital for a merit badge and…:

North interrupted, "She had type O-negative blood."

"Exactly," Vogel exclaimed. "That's not a coincidence."

"Is it possible to talk to the scout leaders for these troops? There's got to be a connection."

"Tracking them down now. I'll ring you back when I've had a chance to talk with them."

"Think you could get dental records for this third girl?"

"Already on it. I'll call back as soon as I get something you can use."

"I appreciate it," North hung up and began scratching notes.

Tiffin looked across the desk impatiently, "Well?"

"No new missing person reports. But," North let the word hang in midair for a moment, "Vogel found a file on a girl missing from a nearby town from about four years ago that seems to tie in with our other two."

"Because she has the same blood type," Tiffin added.

North nodded as he lit a Pall Mall and snapped the lid to the Zippo closed, "And she was also a girl scout whose troop went to the same hospital the others had gone to."

"That's got to be our third girl," Tiffin grabbed a cigarette of his own.

Leaning back in his chair, North mused aloud, "So, all girl scouts with the same blood type who took a trip to the same hospital."

"So the hospital is the connection," Tiffin tossed out.

"Somebody that works at the hospital is the connection."

"That could be a lot of people to sort through."

North took a drag on his cigarette and slowly blew the smoke toward the ceiling, "Even if we rule out orderlies and janitors, there could be hundreds of people who work in a hospital."

Tiffin looked through the dusty Venetian blinds to the street below, "Who would know who had what blood type?"

"I think it's time to call for an expert witness." North picked up the receiver, "Get me Doc Howard."

Chapter 9

Mel Howard took in the information regarding the third missing girl with O-negative blood. "Blood typing is one of the more basic lab tests. Almost every patient will have their blood typed when admitted to the hospital or if they come through the Emergency Room. It's an essential skill to learn if one is going into nursing and easy to teach. I can understand why the scouts would be taught how to do it."

"The question is," North took a pull on his cigarette, "who would have access to their blood types?"

"Well, the lab technician who was teaching them might have noted the information. I could speculate that their scout leaders would know, and of course, the girls themselves."

"Any reason the hospital itself might have kept a record?"

There was a pause on the line, "There was talk a few years ago about collecting people's blood types to help with transfusions if we went to war with Russia. A doctor named Andrew Ivy even suggested that children have their blood types tattooed onto their torso, literally making our children into walking blood banks."

North crushed his cigarette into the ashtray on his desk, "That's insane."

"It was called Operation Tat-Type. Lake County, Indiana, just fifty miles from here, began tattooing blood type onto the left chest of elementary school students in fifty-one. A couple of counties in Utah did the same thing. It only failed because doctors didn't trust tattoos as a source of medical information."

"Holy shit, doc. That sounds like something out of Josef Mengele's playbook."

"Actually, you're close. This Doctor Ivy served in the War and saw that Nazi Storm Troopers had their blood types tattooed on their chests. He brought the idea back to the states."

"So, you're saying it's possible that the hospital collected the girl's blood types as part of some Civil Defense program?"

"That's exactly what I'm saying." Howard lit a cigarette of his own, "A lot of crazy ideas were surfaced in the early days of the Cold War."

"Thanks, Doc. I owe you one."

"I prefer a good Scotch if you're buying," the doctor hung up.

North placed the receiver back onto the cradle of the phone and related the information to Tiffin. "You've got to be kidding me?! Tattoo kids blood types onto them and use them for transfusions?"

"So, what if this hospital in Davenport didn't tattoo the kids?"

Tiffin sat up straight, "But they collected the information for the same purpose. When you need O-negative blood because they're universal donors, you just go and pick up the kids."

North picked up the phone, it was answered by Ruth, "How may I help you, detective?"

"Get the Davenport PD back. I need to speak with Sergeant Joe Vogel."

"I'll ring you back when I have him," the line went dead. North replaced the receiver and walked to Cumming's office to catch him up on the information they had collected so far.

87

Cummings removed the pipe which had been clenched between his teeth, "That's damn good work. Find something to stick Cudlip's murder on this Kelly George, and let me know the instant you hear back from Davenport."

"Gotcha!" North walked back to his desk, "Okay, Tiff. You ready to start looking for witnesses against Machine Gun?"

Tiffin stood and pulled on his overcoat, "Where do you want to start?"

"Let's make the rounds of the bars around Tin City. Someone might know something." North called dispatch to let them know that they would be out of the building. The detectives checked the Mainline out of the motor pool and drove down to the flats. Several bars near the fruit market served the truck drivers and farmers during the summer months. In the dead of winter, the bars were quiet but open.

The Jewel was a bar that saw its first customers in the late nineteenth century. By Christmas of fifty-seven, it had seen better days. The building reeked of stale beer, sweat, and heating oil; Tiffin waved a hand in front of his face.

Half asleep, the aging bartender sat on a chair behind the bar. He startled when the bell over the door rang, "What can I do for you?" he asked as he stood.

North reached into his pocket and pulled out the booking photo of Kelly George, "You recognize this man?"

"Yeah, calls himself Machine Gun. I call him a bum. He's not welcome here."

"Why's that?" North lit a cigarette.

"He's picked one too many fights."

"When was the last time he was here?" Tiffin asked.

"Six months, maybe more. Like I said, he's not welcome here. Now, if you boys ain't buying, I'm done talking," the bartender sat back down on the stool he had been occupying.

Their next stop was Babe's Lounge down by the canal. "Look, guys," Babe said as the detectives showed him George's photo, "I run a class joint. I don't allow floaters or vagrants in; it's bad for business."

Tiffin looked at the picture, then at Babe, "How can you tell he's a floater by this picture?"

Babe gave a hearty laugh, "I've kicked his sorry ass out of here a few times. I know exactly what kind of man he is."

"Yeah, what's that?" North asked.

"He's a loser who thinks he's a big shot. Bad combination, if you know what I mean."

It was at their third stop, the UnderTow Bar, that they found George's favorite watering hole, "Yeah, a barmaid said, Machine Gun was in here last Saturday night. Ran out on his tab, and I got stuck with the bill."

North jotted a few notes, "Was he alone or with somebody?"

"He was talking to Baxter," she nodded toward a floater seated in the corner nursing a beer. "That's him there."

Tiffin and North walked up to the middle-aged man. It was evident by his yellow pallor and enlarged gut that this was not Baxter's first beer. Tiffin stood behind him as North approached from the front, "Your name's Baxter, is it?"

"I ain't done nothing," the floater lowered the beer glass to the table.

"Didn't say you did. I hear you were talking with Kelly George Saturday night."

"Well, I was talking to Machine Gun alright, just don't know what night it was. Hell, I don't know what today is."

"But you do remember talking to him?" North asked, trying not to sound irritated.

"Oh yeah, we talked a lot."

"He happen to mention a guy by the name of Mack Cudlip?"

"Yeah. Machine Gun said Cudlip owed him three bucks but only had forty cents on him," Baxter took a sip of obviously warm beer.

North looked past Baxter to Tiffin, "George told you that Cudlip only had forty cents on him? When was that?"

"When we was talking the other night."

"No, did George tell you when it was that Cudlip had only forty cents on him?"

"Nah. But he said he had to dig through Cudlip's pockets to find four dimes."

"Is Baxter your first name or your last?" Tiffin asked from behind the man.

"Bobby is my Christian name."

"Bobby Baxter," North began, "I'm taking you in as a witness in the case against Kelly George."

"Why are you arresting me? I ain't done nothing wrong."

"Do you have a permanent address?" North asked as he handcuffed the floater.

"Nah. I ain't got no regular address."

"Then, I'm guessing the judge will give you an address at the county jail until George's court date." North looked at the barmaid, "What does our friend here owe you for the beer?"

She looked at the detectives "Two bits."

90

North handed her a half-dollar, "Baxter wants you to have a nice tip."

Tiffin turned to the barmaid, "I need your name and address for our report."

"I really don't want to be involved. I didn't see anything," the young blonde said plaintively.

"I still need the information."

"Dolly Chapman," Tiffin scratched notes onto his pad. "I live with my aunt at five forty-seven McAlister. Can you arrest Mr. Baxter for being a witness?"

"We're not arresting him. We're holding him as a witness." North tipped the Stetson in her direction, "Thank you for your help.

The detectives took Baxter to the county jail and signed him in as a witness. Back at the Safety Building, they caught the Chief up and returned a call to Vogel in Davenport. "Yes, I need you to go to the hospital and check to see if they're maintaining records of who has what blood type. Then find out who has access to that information," North paused to take a drag on his cigarette as he listened to Vogel complain about the work, "Yes, I've been told that I'm a pain in the ass," pause. "Okay, thank you. I appreciate your help."

Tiffin peered across the desk, "Well?"

"Vogel is going to check with Mercy Hospital, and he's not happy about it."

"Not even if it helps him close a couple of open cases?" Tiffin shrugged. "What next?"

North looked at the Simplex clock on the wall, "I think it's time for lunch."

Tiffin looked at the clock; it was a quarter of twelve, "I couldn't agree more."

91

Roxy began pouring beer the moment that North and Tiffin walked into the Trophy Room, "Hey Brick, hey Tiff. What'll it be other than your usual?"

"Have Charlie drop a burger with grilled onions for me," Tiffin called over his shoulder as the detectives took a table in the corner. Tiffin tossed his overcoat and hat on the empty chair next to the one on which he sat. North pulled off his suit jacket and hat. He adjusted the worn leather shoulder holster as he sat down.

Roxy sat their drinks down in front of them. North held a finger in the air, indicating for her to wait as he tossed the shot of whiskey back. He handed her the empty shot glass.

"Still a pretty weak case against Charles," Tiffin sipped his beer.

"It's a start. The waitress can place him having a conversation with Baxter. Baxter can explain how Charles told him that he'd dug through Cudlip's pockets."

"And there's nothing that places Charles with Cudlip."

North took a deep drink of the beer, "My dad used to say that if you took care of the big stuff, the details would work themselves out."

"So, we're only sweating a few details?"

"Sure, Tiff." North downed the rest of the beer, "Only a few details."

"How long do you figure we have to get these details put together?"

"With the holidays, I bet we can buy ourselves ten days. Maybe two weeks if the acting DA is generous."

Roxy handed North another whiskey and brought both of them another beer when she brought Tiffin's burger. Tiffin, thinking about his pocketbook, looked up, "I didn't order another beer."

92

"Don't worry, Tiff, that one's on the house. Think of it as my Christmas present to you two." With that, the co-owner of the Trophy Room turned to help another patron who had just entered the bar. Tiffin began to sip at the complimentary glass of beer.

There was a message from Vogel waiting for them when they returned to the squad room. North read it and passed the paper across to Tiffin, "So, they were keeping records of people's blood types." He handed the note back to North.

"Damn," North exclaimed. "I really need to be in Davenport to interview the staff at Mercy Hospital."

"I'm sure Vogel can take care of that," Tiffin looked at North, who clearly disagreed with his statement.

Shaking his head, North walked into the chief's office, "I need to take a day off."

Cummings looked none too pleased, "You just got back to work."

"There's a definite connection between these bodies that were found at the Cooper Wells building and Davenport. I'm going to fly there and try to get the pieces to fit together."

"I don't have the budget for you to fly to Iowa. So it's out of the question."

"I'll pay for my own travel and do it on my own time. I'm just asking for tomorrow off," North reached into his pocket and pulled out a cigarette and his lighter.

Cummings fumed, "And if I say no?"

"I think I feel sick. I'll probably need to take tomorrow off."

"And you're back here Monday morning?"

"All bright-eyed and bushy-tailed."

"Go!"

"To Davenport?"

"At the moment, just get out of my office." North shut the door behind him as he left.

He picked up his desk phone, "How may I help you, detective?"

"Get me the ticket counter at Lakeland Airport."

"I'll call you back when I have them on the line."

A minute later, the phone rang, "Detective North."

"Hold for the ticket counter." There were a couple of clicks on the line, "Lakeland Airport, how may I help you?"

"I need to be in Davenport, Iowa, by tomorrow morning. How can you get me there?"

"Let me check flight schedules. What time do you need to be in Davenport?"

North lit a cigarette, "As early as possible."

There was a pause, "I can get you on an Eastern flight out of here at six tomorrow morning. You'll change planes in Chicago and be in Davenport by nine their time."

"Yeah, that'll work."

"When do you want to return?"

"Can you get me back on Saturday?"

There was a pause as the ticket agent checked the flight schedule book, "I can get you out of Davenport Saturday at noon. Change planes in Chicago and have you back here at five o'clock."

"Okay, that's fine. How much is this excursion going to set me back?"

"Let me do the math," again, there was a pause. "One hundred and twenty-seven dollars."

"Great, book me on those flights."

"Your name, sir?"

"Richard North."

"Is this a business trip or pleasure?"

North wanted to ask who would go to Davenport for pleasure but held back on the sarcasm, "Business."

"What company do you represent?"

"LaSalle Harbor PD."

There was a brief pause, "You're Brick North, is that correct? I've heard a lot about you."

North recalled how Lucky Como's luck had run out at Lakeland and how the tall, buxom, and confident brunette who now managed the airport had saved his life. "Guilty as charged," he finally answered.

"I'll let Miss Arquette know you'll be traveling through Lakeland."

He began to say that it wouldn't be necessary but was cut off as the ticket agent interrupted, "Excuse me, I have another call coming in. We'll see you in the morning."

North looked at the receiver for a moment before hanging it up. "I need to go to the bank and get some cash," he said to Tiffin before pulling on his jacket and hat. "I'll be back soon."

"So, the chief gave you permission to go?" Tiffin asked with an air of doubt to his voice.

"He didn't not give me permission," North said as he walked to the stairs.

Tiffin shook his head and began to type up the notes he had made on the morning's work.

Chapter 10

North left his house at a quarter past five. The evening before, he'd arranged with the Wolfe boys to take care of Gatto; Adele seemed very happy to see him at her door. The boys, who had never been farther than twenty miles from LaSalle Harbor, were amazed to think that one could drop everything and travel so far at the spur of the moment.

Eastern Air Line's twin-engine Martin 404 was sitting on the runway outside the terminal being gassed up as North pulled the Dodge into a parking stall at Lakeland Airport. He joined a handful of other passengers at the ticket counter. "Your name, sir?" the young woman asked as he approached the counter.

"Richard North."

"Hello, Brick," a breathy voice said from behind.

He turned to see Suzette standing ten feet away. She looked every bit as good as when he had last seen her. "Hello, Suzette, good to see you," small talk was not North's strong point.

"It's been six months since we were last in the building together. How've you been?"

"I've been good. How about you?"

"Busy. This place has a lot of paperwork to keep me occupied. You look good." Suzette paused for a moment before voicing the question she was aching to ask, "The girl who stole your heart, she still around?"

North looked down, "No, she got sick a few months ago and didn't make it."

Suzette put a hand on North's arm, "Oh, Brick. I'm so sorry. What was it?"

"Something called meningitis. It took her quickly."

"I feel terrible for having asked. Please forgive me."

"Nothing to forgive. You couldn't have known," North pulled the pack of cigarettes from his pocket.

"You can't smoke in here anymore," the ticket agent cautioned, "the Civil Aeronautics Administration has banned smoking in the terminal. You'll need to wait until you're on the plane."

North shook his head and pushed the Pall Malls back into his jacket pocket.

"So," Suzette worked at changing the subject, "what takes you to Davenport?"

"Police business. Nothing exotic."

"I saw that you're due back tomorrow at five. You have any plans for Saturday night?" if anything, Suzette's words were breathier than usual.

North looked down into her dark eyes, "Nothing specific."

"Perhaps we could grab a drink or something," she looked away demurely.

"Sure, doll. That would be great." North traded cash for the tickets and thanked the agent behind the counter as he stuffed the change into his trouser pocket.

"I'll see you here when you get back," Suzette squeezed his arm before she turned and walked toward the corridor that led to her office. Her heel-to-toe gait accentuated the movement of her hips.

North handed his bag to the cargo handler at the foot of the steps leading up to the plane and accepted the claim check. Ducking as he entered the aluminum tube that would take him to Chicago, he looked at his ticket for the seat assignment. Finding his seat, he strapped himself in; the stewardess approached, "This is a short flight, so there's no meal service. But as soon as we're airborne, I'll bring you a beverage. What would you like?"

"Bourbon," North replied as he studied the attractive young woman who stood over him.

The stewardess, nonplussed, smiled, "Do you want a pop to go with that or on the rocks?"

"Just bourbon in a glass will be fine." North began reading the propaganda Eastern left in the seat pocket in front of him. Within minutes the door at the front of the cabin was closed, and the stewardess took her jump seat near the door. The plane taxied to the eastern edge of the runway, turned west, and waited for clearance from the tower. With the brakes securely locked, the pilot revved the pair of piston engines. As the plane began to shudder, the brakes were released. The Martin 404 launched itself down the runway and into the prevailing winds off Lake Michigan. The seventeen-ton plane pulled itself up and over the waters.

A little over fifty minutes after they left LaSalle Harbor, the plane touched down at Midway Airport on the south side of Chicago. North picked up his bag at the foot of the stairs as he exited the plane and walked into the terminal. Much larger and busier than Lakeland, Midway had twenty gates. It took North a few moments to find a skycap who could help direct him where to go. "Let me see your ticket, sir," the skycap asked. North handed him his ticket.

"Okay, the flight to Moline is departing out of gate eleven." The worker pointed down the terminal, "It'll be on your right, sir."

"Moline?!" North jumped, "I'm supposed to be going to Davenport."

"Yes, sir. The Moline, Illinois, airport serves Davenport, Moline, and Rock Island. So you're going to the right place."

North took a half-dollar out of his pocket and tossed it to the skycap, "Appreciate your help."

The skycap looked at the coin and tipped his cap, "Thank you, sir. Thank you very much."

With the change from Eastern to Central Time, North had arrived in Chicago at about six o'clock. His flight to Davenport, or Moline, or wherever he was going, would not board for almost two hours.

He wandered the terminal for a few minutes before he found a place where he could get some breakfast. "Would you like to see a menu?" a middle-aged waitress asked as she approached with a white mug and a pot of coffee as he sat down at an open table.

"No. Just bring me some fried potatoes and a couple eggs over hard. Oh, and toast with no butter."

"That'll come with your choice of meat. Do you want sausage, bacon, or ham?"

She began to pour coffee into the mug as he thought, "Sausage is fine."

He picked up a copy of the Chicago Sun-Times that another patron left sitting on a table; he leafed through it as he ate his breakfast.

The flight to Moline was as uneventful as the one to Chicago had been. The only difference was instead of waves, the view out of the window was that of fields.

North grabbed his bag from the cargo worker at the foot of the stairs and walked across the tarmac and into the terminal. Vogel was supposed to be meeting him, but North had no idea of what the Davenport police officer looked like. Standing near a payphone was a police officer; North walked over, "You Vogel?"

"I'm Sergeant Vogel," the officer who stood a good eight inches shorter than North said. "You must be North."

"If we're standing on formality, I'm Detective Lieutenant North. Unless you plan on calling me by my title for however many hours we're together, I'll call you Vogel, and you can call me North. Does that work for you?"

A little less cocky, Vogel stuck out his hand, "Call me Joe."

North gripped the offered hand, "Most everyone calls me Brick."

"The car's out front." Vogel led the way out of the terminal and to a black police car parked at the curb. North's bag secured in the trunk, they made their way across the Mississippi and into Davenport. Brick was thankful that Vogel had as little time for small talk as he did. Fifteen minutes after leaving the airport, they parked at the curb in front of Mercy Hospital.

North crushed the Stetson over his mop of wavy hair while Vogel straightened his eight-point service hat on his head. They walked into the imposing red brick building and were met by one of the Sisters of Mercy who ran the hospital, dressed in her black habit and white whimple, "How may I assist you, gentlemen?"

Vogel deferred to North, who removed his hat, "I'm Detective Richard North of the LaSalle Harbor, Michigan, Police Department; this is Sergeant Joe Vogel from the Davenport PD. We have few questions about information that may have been collected regarding individuals and their blood types."

"We treat patient information with the utmost confidentiality."

"And we appreciate that. However, I'm investigating the murders of three girls and the possibility that they were targeted because they'd participated in a program at this hospital."

The sister looked between North and Vogel, "I think we should speak with Mother Superior." She turned and began walking toward a bank of elevators. "Please keep up, gentlemen," she called over her shoulder.

North was surprised the elevator took them to the basement level instead of one of the upper floors, "Your superior's office is in the basement?"

"We don't think of it as a basement. It's the lower level, and the administration office is here. It is a sign of humility." A few paces from the elevator, the sister knocked on a simple wooden door.

"Come forward," a voice came through the door. The sister opened the door, then stepped out of the way for them to enter. "How may I help you, gentlemen?" the older nun asked.

After introducing themselves, North began, "We've found the remains of three teenage girls. In the course of our investigation, we learned that each girl was from the Davenport area, each girl belonged to a scout troop, and each came here with their troop to learn about blood typing."

"We, of course, are terribly distressed to learn of the fate of these young women," the head sister began. "However, as it sounds as if you already know of their connection with Mercy Hospital, I am at a loss as to how we may further assist you."

"We know that many hospitals worked with the local Civil Defense authorities to collect information about donors in the event of war."

With her elbows on her desk and her hands clasped in front of her face, she took on a controlled tone, "Let me be as straightforward as possible. Our records are not open to public inspection."

"We do not wish to see your records," North looked for an ashtray. Not seeing one, he continued, "We do wish to know who would have access to them."

The Mother Superior sat quietly for a moment, "We did indeed collect blood information for the Civil Defense beginning in forty-nine. It was discontinued in fifty-five."

North tried to be patient, a trait he was not known for. "Do those records still exist?"

"I do believe that information is in our archives."

Vogel spoke up. "Mother Superior," he began.

"You may address me as Reverend Mother," the sister uttered stiffly.

The Sergeant cleared his throat, "Reverend Mother, you are taking this conversation in circles."

"Are you accusing me of obfuscating?"

"Whether you are doing so deliberately or not," North looked into her eyes, "the answer is yes. This is a police matter, and you are standing in the way of our investigation. So I will ask you again, and I would like an answer this time, who has access to those records?"

Before answering, the sister took a deep breath, "The archives are not open to the general staff. They are primarily used by our physicians to provide improved care for our patients and to conduct research."

"Where are the archives located," Vogel asked.

"At the far end of this corridor," she used her hand to point to the right.

"Is the archive locked?" North asked.

The sister shook her head, "There is no need to lock the room. The file cabinets themselves are locked. One must sign the register to access the keys."

"May we see the archive and the register, please?" North asked as politely as he was capable of.

Hesitantly, the sister finally stood, "Follow me, gentlemen." She led them down the hallway. They stood in front of another simple wooden door. An etched brass sign next to the door read, "Archive." The sister opened the door and flicked the light switch. In front of them was a table with a register book. Next to the book was a ring of keys. North suspected that each key fit one of the dozens of file cabinets in the room.

North was stunned, "Are those the keys to the filing cabinets?"

"Yes," the sister responded, "one signs the register to indicate which file they are accessing. It works quite well."

Vogel looked around the room in disbelief, "So anyone could come in here and look at whatever they want?"

"Where are the blood type records stored?" North tried to get them back on track.

"Cabinet fourteen."

North picked up the register, flipped back to nineteen fifty, and began running his finger down the column which indicated file cabinet numbers. As he found a name for cabinet fourteen, he called out the name to Vogel, who was making notes, "John Cantwell, William Foley, Robert Jameson, Leo Miltner, James Dunn, Gerald Doolen, William Harkness, James Porter." Some of the names had looked at the file many times over five years; others only once. Finally, he looked to the sister, "Do you know any of these names?"

"They're all doctors except William Foley, who was with the Civil Defense."

"It doesn't look like anyone has looked into the file in at least two years."

She answered defensively, "I wouldn't know about that."

Taking the notepad from Vogel, North read the names aloud to the sister, "Cantwell, Jameson, Miltner, Dunn, Doolen, Harkness, and Porter. They're doctors?"

"Yes."

"Are they all still practicing medicine?"

"Doctor Porter died three years ago from pneumonia. May God rest his soul."

North scratched through the name, "And the others?"

"Doctors Doolen and Jameson have both given up their hospital privileges within the past two years."

"Do you have contact information for any or all of them?"

"I have their information in my office," She pulled the door open and led them back to her office. Once inside, she opened a drawer in her desk and pulled out a manila folder. "Are you prepared to write this down?" she asked in such a way to remind North of a teacher asking an elementary student. Sarcastically he answered, "Yes, ma'am."

"Dr. Cantwell's office is in the First National Bank building. The number is 2-3961. Dr. Miltner is in the Davenport Bank building; 2-2164. Dr. Dunn is also in the Davenport Bank building; 2-2037. Finally, Dr. Harkness is at 2410 River; 3-2253." Vogel and North both scratched notes.

North turned to Vogel, "Two and three represent what exchanges?"

105

"Two is ACademy, three is IDlewood."

North added to his notes. "Any information on either Doolen or Jameson?"

"No, I am afraid that I do not. I know that neither doctor retained their private practice after they left the hospital."

Vogel looked at the sister, "So, they both retired?"

"I believe that is what I have just told you." The sister sat down behind her desk and looked at North and Vogel for a moment, "I think our conversation has reached its conclusion."

The two men turned toward the door. North began to pull the door open when a thought came to him, "Reverend Mother, one final question."

"What is it?" her irritation showing.

"Were any of these doctors part of the blood type collection program?"

"Doctor Jameson headed the project and worked closely with Mr. Foley," She looked down at a pile of papers on her desk. "Now, good day."

In the lobby, Vogel walked over to a payphone and opened the directory. "Okay, let's see, here he is; Doolen, Gerald MD. His Residence is 1928 Fernwood. Number 2-4298." North made notes as Vogel looked up the other retired physician. "And, Jameson, Robert MD. He lives at 2728 Davenport. The number there is 2-8892."

"What say we start with Jameson? He led the project for the hospital," North clicked the lid to his Zippo shut.

"Okay. Jameson, it is. Davenport avenue is fairly close." The drive from the hospital took only five minutes. The Jameson house was a two-story bungalow. The white clapboard house with green trim reminded North of his parent's cottage in Hell.

Vogel rang the doorbell; North stood at the bottom of the three steps which led up to the stoop. The door was answered by an older, balding man, "May I help you, gentlemen?"

"Doctor Jameson?" Vogel asked politely.

"Yes?"

"I'm Sergeant Vogel of the Davenport police, and this is Detective North from the LaSalle Harbor, Michigan police. May we speak with you for a moment?"

"What's this about?" Jameson seemed puzzled.

North spoke up, "We have a couple of questions about the blood type project you oversaw for the local Office of Civil Defense."

"Oh, that ended several years ago."

"We understand that. Here's the issue, it seems that several teenaged girls who were typed ended up dead two hundred and fifty miles away in Michigan," North watched the doctor's eyes which showed surprise. "Perhaps we could come in and speak with you."

Jameson stepped aside and let Vogel and North into his home. "You say several girls. How many are we talking about?"

North sat on a brocade chair and lit a cigarette, "We have the remains of three girls, all in their mid-teens. Surprisingly, all with the same blood type."

"O-negative, correct?"

"How did you know that?" Vogel asked with an edge to his voice.

"As you may be aware," the doctor paused to light his own cigarette, "people with O-negative blood are considered universal donors."

North nodded, "Yes. I know that."

"If we found ourselves fighting an invading Soviet army, there may not be time to find a matching donor. So let's say you find someone who has AB-negative blood, which accounts for maybe one percent of the population, or B-negative at two percent; our universal donors would be a Godsend."

North scratched a few notes, "So, you paid special attention to that particular blood type?"

"Yes, we kept careful watch on our O-negs."

"And you had scout troops come in to learn how to type blood as a way of identifying donors."

"Scout troops, high school biology classes, national guardsmen. We got creative in recruiting people to the program. Of course, the Red Cross helped provide names and addresses of their donors."

Vogel gave Jameson a stern look, "Did you ever work directly with any of those who came in to learn to type their blood?"

"No," the doctor said confidently, "I worked with Mr. Foley from the Office of Civil Defense and was charged with maintaining the records."

"Did you ever go through the records searching for a particular person or persons?" North interjected.

"W-Why would I do that?"

"Forgive us, doctor," Vogel put a hand on North's shoulder and pulled him back. "Thank you for your time."

North exploded the moment the front door closed behind them, "What the hell, Joe? Put a hand on my shoulder like that again, and I'll tear it off your arm."

"He didn't do it. Did you see how he reacted to your questions? He was answering you honestly."

"So what, now you're a fucking lie detector?"

Vogel fired up the car, "Do you think he's guilty?"

"No, but that doesn't mean he doesn't know something that could have been helpful. Believe it or not, Sergeant, I know my job. Now, step back and let me do it."

"What's next, Lieutenant?"

"Next, let's get back to first names. Then, let's look up the two doctors that both have offices in that bank building," North lit a cigarette and picked a piece of loose tobacco off his lip.

Chapter 11

Both Doctor Miltner and Doctor Dunn were open about their work in the archives. "I visited a few times," Miltner explained. "I knew Civil Defense had taken an interest in blood typing, and I was curious about how many names they had on file."

"Why curious, Doctor," North asked as they stood in a small examination room.

"I found the whole program to be dangerous because of its secrecy."

North shook his head, "So you invaded people's privacy by looking through the records?"

"I wasn't interested in names. I was interested in numbers. We're a community of eighty-nine thousand people, and we had managed to collect blood types on almost eleven thousand of them without their knowledge. I was collecting numbers that I later used to argue with the hospital board and the Civil Defense Office."

"So, you don't think it's a good idea to be prepared against a Soviet invasion," Vogel asked.

"I don't think that anything done in secret is good. I believe the people involved needed to know that they could possibly be picked up and have their blood taken by force if necessary."

Vogel seemed agitated, "Certainly Civil Defense wouldn't take people against their will to be tapped for their blood."

Miltner lit a cigarette, "You're joking, right? The Red Scare is alive and well in the heartland of America, especially here in Iowa. Farmers are literally whitewashing barns that have been painted red for generations."

"So, you don't think there's a common good that this program helped secure?" Vogel demanded.

The doctor looked Vogel in the eye, "You married?"

"Yeah, so…"

"You got kids?"

Vogel looked more confused than agitated, "Yeah. So what's your point?"

"Suppose you come home from work tonight and your kids are alone because the Civil Defense has come and taken your wife."

"That wouldn't happen," Vogel argued.

"And you're naive if you think the government you work for wouldn't sacrifice a housewife if some general who was important to the war effort needed blood. Now, gentlemen, if you'll excuse me, I have patients to see."

Back in the car, Vogel rolled his wrist over and looked at his watch, "You want to grab some lunch?"

North looked at his own watch, "What do you have in mind?"

"There's a place down the street that we can get us a loose meat sandwich."

"I have no idea what this is." North lit a cigarette, "But if they can fix me up with a bump and a beer, I'll be good."

Vogel gave North an odd look, "You normally drink on duty?"

"Two points," North took a deep pull on his cigarette and slowly let the smoke out, "I'm not on duty now, nor am I on duty when I'm at lunch."

"Well, I'm in uniform and couldn't have one if I wanted to."

Vogel parked the police car in the alley behind a row of buildings and led North through the back door of one of the buildings. They found themselves inside a narrow bar, not unlike the Trophy Room back home.

The bartender looked up as the two of them entered, "Hey, Joe. What'll it be?"

"Howdy, Phil. I'll have a loose meat sandwich and a 7-Up. My friend here wants a bump and a beer."

The bartender looked at North, "You particular about either your whiskey or your beer?"

North smiled, just the corner of his lip rising, "Nope, as long as they're both cheap."

"You want a sandwich?" Vogel asked.

"Not usually," North picked up his beverages from the bartop and walked to a table in the rear of the room, placing his back firmly against the wall.

Vogel took a sip of his soda, "How long have you been a cop?"

"Eleven years," North tossed back the whiskey and held the shot glass up until he saw the bartender nod. "How about you; how long have you been a cop?"

"Since I was separated from the Navy in 47, so a little over ten years."

The bartender carried a plate with Vogel's sandwich and another shot of whiskey to the table. North looked at the sandwich, "What the hell is that?"

"Loose meat," Vogel said as he took a bite of the sandwich. It seemed to North that half the dry ground meat fell out of the bun and onto the plate.

North pulled out his notepad and looked at the names and addresses of the three doctors they still hadn't spoken with, "Okay, Harkness in on River, Cantwell is in the First National Bank building, and Doolan lives on Fernwood. Where to first?"

Vogel sucked meat from the bun before it fell to the plate, "The bank building is only a couple of blocks from here. River Avenue is between there and Fernwood."

Doctor Cantwell's office was on the third floor of the First National Bank building. The young nurse seated behind the desk appeared surprised when a uniformed police officer opened the door, "How may I help you, officer?"

"We'd like to speak with Doctor Cantwell for a moment, please," Vogel responded.

"I'm afraid that is not possible."

"Why's that?" North asked.

"The doctor is making house calls this afternoon." She looked past Vogel and admiringly at North, "Perhaps there's something I can do for you?"

North grinned, "When do you expect him back?"

"I would think between three and three-thirty." The nurse consulted the schedule on her desk, "He has an appointment here at four."

Vogel placed his uniform cap on his head, "We'll be back at three-thirty. Thank you for your help."

"Three down and still three to go," North said as he slid into the patrol car.

"Let's cut that down. Let's see what Dr. Harkness has to say," Vogel pushed the gear shift on the steering column into first and slowly let the clutch out. Within five minutes, they were at the River street address. The front of the stately three-story Craftsman home had been converted into the doctor's offices. North rang the bell, and they waited. Within a minute, the door was answered by an older woman dressed in a white nurse's uniform.

"Is there something I can help you with?"

Vogel and North removed their hats. "We have a few questions for Doctor Harkness," Vogel said matter-of-factly.

"The doctor is with a patient, and we have another patient waiting to see him."

This was one of those times that North would typically have turned on the charm. However, something about the nurse's demeanor told him charm would be wasted upon her. "Perhaps we can have a minute with him between patients."

"What is this concerning?" the nurse said through pursed lips.

North gave a stern look, "It concerns a police investigation."

The nurse looked like she had something to say but instead stood down, "Please wait out here. I will send the doctor out when he is free." The door closed behind her.

"She's friendly," North said sarcastically as he lit a Pall Mall.

"I was reading about a new musical that just opened on Broadway," Vogel lit a cigarette of his own. "There's a line that says, 'There's nothing halfway about the Iowa way to treat you, when we treat you, which we may not do at all.'"

"That's from a musical, you say?"

114

"It was quoted in an editorial in the Quad-City Times. The editor felt it was a slap-in-the-face to Iowans. I happen to think it's right on the money."

North chuckled, "Well, if the nurse here is an example of the typical Iowan, I'd say you're right."

"I think it has a lot to do with the stoic German background of so many of those who live here."

"Vogel, that's German, isn't it," North picked a piece of loose tobacco off his lip.

"Well, there are Germans, and then there are Germans," Vogel laughed.

They had just finished their cigarettes when Doctor Harkness stepped out following an attractive young woman whom North took to be his patient. "I'm Doctor Harkness. How may I help you?"

"I'm Sergeant Vogel from the Davenport PD; this is Detective North from LaSalle Harbor, Michigan. May we ask you a couple of questions?"

"Certainly." The doctor looked at North, "You're a long way from home."

"Three bodies have been found in LaSalle Harbor. They all appear to have ties to Davenport and Mercy Hospital."

"I don't understand how I can help you."

Vogel stepped in, "We're talking to all those who had access to the blood type records being maintained by the hospital. You accessed the records several times over the past few years."

The doctor lit a cigarette, "Yes, I did."

"May we ask why you needed to do so?" North felt like he was pulling teeth with both the nurse and the doctor.

"I was working with a leukemia patient and was looking for a steady supply of donors with AB-negative blood."

"Why not use O-negative donors?" North lit another cigarette.

"Universal donors are acceptable in an emergency, but it's always best if we can transfuse with an exact match. Why the interest in the blood type program?"

"It seems that all of our victims were taught to type blood at Mercy Hospital."

Harkness looked between North and Vogel, "The hospital brought hundreds of people through to collect blood types. So what's the significance?"

North took a drag on his cigarette before he answered, "These were teenaged girls all with type O-negative blood. Do you believe in coincidences, doctor?"

"As a general rule, no, I don't."

"Neither do I. So, I'm going to ask you bluntly, why would someone kidnap three girls that had each been through the hospital program, and each had the same blood type?"

"I-I don't have an answer to that."

"But, it's no coincidence."

"No," the doctor looked shaken. "It's no coincidence."

"Speculate."

The doctor looked at North for a moment while he thought, "Were all the girls taken at once or over some time?"

"Perhaps one a year over three years."

"Someone wanted a fresh blood supply?" the doctor wondered.

"We'd also come up with that idea. Hemophilia or some other blood disorder was suggested by a doctor back home."

The doctor thought for a moment, "Cancer, like my leukemia patient, and liver or kidney patients often need transfusions." He smoked his cigarette, "Perhaps anemia or a severe infection."

North gave the doctor a quizzical look, "Help us rule some of these out. could someone have any of these diseases and live four or five years?"

"Anemia, perhaps," the doctor took another drag on his cigarette. "Cirrhosis of the liver is helped sometimes by a transfusion, but cirrhosis patients don't live that long. Twenty-five percent of liver disease patients develop esophageal varices and may begin to bleed out; transfusions will help them temporarily, but the mortality rate is nearly one hundred percent. Patients with renal failure also have a limited life span. Again, a transfusion will help, but it's temporary help."

North crushed his cigarette out on the step and field stripped the butt before shoving it into his pant pocket, "So, no one with a disease that requires a blood transfusion could live four or five years?"

"There are always exceptions. For example, someone under intense medical care might be able to live with any of these diseases."

"How intensive would this care need to be?"

Harkness shook his head, "More intense than any hospital could provide. We'd be talking about round-the-clock care."

North tipped his hat, "Thank you, Doc, you've been very helpful." Then, back in the car, he looked at his Bulova, "It's only a quarter past two. Shall we visit Doolen before we head back to Cantwell?"

Vogel nodded and looked at his notes, "1928 Fernwood Avenue; it's out toward the edge of town. Won't take too long to get there." He turned the car west and headed out Locust Street. Within ten minutes,

117

they were walking up the sidewalk. "Nice house," Vogel said as he rang the bell.

A middle-aged woman answered the door, "Police?! Has something happened to Henry?"

Vogel took off his hat, "We're looking to speak with Doctor Gerald Doolen."

"Doctor Doolen sold us this house just last month. I'm Mrs. Plath, Lois Plath. My husband, Henry, is one of the principals at Holst Monument on Fairmount."

"Did the Doolen's leave a forwarding address?" North tried to mask his frustration.

"No. Doctor Doolen said that they were moving to some town in Southwest Michigan. Unfortunately, I don't recall the name."

"LaSalle Harbor," North didn't phrase it as a question.

"I'm sure that's it," Mrs. Plath exclaimed. "I'm certain. He said someone in his wife's family had left them a house there."

Chapter 12

Vogel dropped North off at the Mississippi Hotel at the corner of Third and Brady. The hotel was reminiscent of the Swanson in LaSalle Harbor, where North had lodged for two years. The primary difference was that each room in the Mississippi had a private bath. North picked up the phone, "Hotel Operator," a nasal voice answered.

"This is Mr. North in room four seventeen. I need you to connect me with the Police Department in LaSalle Harbor, Michigan."

"The hotel does charge a surcharge for long-distance calls placed through our switchboard."

North clicked the lid to his Zippo closed, "Yeah, I understand."

"I will ring you when I've made the connection."

"Can you transfer me to Room Service?"

"One moment, please."

After asking for a bottle of bourbon to be sent to his room, North leaned back on the bed. It had been a long day. He hadn't realized that he'd drifted off until the telephone ringing and a knock on the door happened simultaneously. He grabbed the doorknob and pulled the door open as he answered the phone. He nodded toward the table, indicating where the bellman could set the tray with its pint bottle of liquor and two glasses. He tossed the bellman a half-dollar, as he said, "North" into the receiver.

"Please hold for your call," there was a couple of clicks on the line before a familiar voice said, "LaSalle Harbor Police Department, how may I help you?"

"Ruth? It's Brick North."

"Brick! Where are you? The operator I spoke with said this was a long-distance call."

"Ha! Davenport, Iowa. I need to speak with Detective Tiffin. Is he still in the building?"

"I believe he is. Please hold while I transfer your call." Then in a soft voice, "Hurry home."

There were the customary clicks. The phone rang several times before it was answered, "Detective Tiffin."

"Tiff, it's Brick. Glad you're still there."

"I was halfway down the stairs when I heard the phone ring. Thought it might be you, so I answered. You find anything?"

"Grab a pencil and write the name down," North paused for a moment. "Ready?"

"Yeah, what've you got?"

"Dr. Gerald Doolen."

Tiffin scratched the name on his desk blotter, "Who's that?"

"A doctor who retired from the hospital here and moved to LaSalle Harbor."

"No shit? That's huge. You have any contact information for him?"

"That's the hangup with all of this," North pulled the cork from the bottle and poured a couple of fingers into the rocks glass the bellman had brought with him.

"What kind of hangup?"

"According to the woman who bought Doolen's house, they were moving to a place that his wife's family had left them. So the property might not be in his name."

Tiffin shook his head and plopped down in his chair, "Crap. That is a problem."

Looking at his watch, North saw that it was a quarter past five in Michigan, "The county records office is closed, so we'll have to wait until Monday to talk to them. But, you might check with the chief and see if he'll free up a few uni's to knock on doors on the lakefront and the bluff and see if anyone knows the Doolens."

"Why the lakefront and the bluff. They could be anywhere in the city or beyond?"

"Where were the bodies found?" North took a sip of the bourbon.

"At the old Cooper Wells building."

"And what neighborhoods are closest to there?"

"Ah! Got it." Tiffin paused to light a cigarette, "When are you back?"

"Five o'clock tomorrow afternoon."

"Okay. Good work! I'll check with the boss and see what he thinks about going door-to-door."

"Thanks, Tiff," North hung up the phone and tossed back the bourbon. It was much smoother than the Old Quaker he was used to. He looked at the label on the bottle, "Four Roses," he said to himself. "Good stuff."

With a couple of drinks and a nap under his belt, North wandered down to the hotel's restaurant on the first floor. After having convinced both the waiter and the cook that, yes, he really did want his steak that rare, he had supper.

It was a chilly thirty-five degrees when he stepped out onto Brady Street and crushed the Stetson onto his head. North lit a cigarette and began walking down the street toward the Mississippi River. On a Friday evening, the only thing open were some bars near the river. He stepped into the Riverside Bar and grabbed an empty stool.

"What'll it be, Mac?" the bartender asked.

"Fix me up with a bump and a beer," North said as he surveyed the building and its clientele.

The bartender stood looking at North, "Fifty cents."

"I'm accustomed to paying for things once I've received them," North lit a cigarette and picked a piece of loose tobacco off his lip.

"Look, Mac, I'll pour your drinks when you've paid for them. That's how it works. Don't need someone dead-beating me on their drinks. Now it's going to be a buck if you want it."

North narrowed his eyes and looked at the bartender, "Bring my drinks, put them on the bar, and I'll pay you the fifty cents. That's how this is going to work."

A man who had been seated at a table near the door stood and walked over, "Is there a problem here, Kevin?"

"Sorry, Mr. O'Clery, but this guy doesn't understand how we do business."

"Okay, Bub. Maybe you just didn't understand what Kevin here was telling you. Pay him a dollar, and he'll get your drink for you. Simply enough."

North took a pull on his cigarette and leaned on the bar, not looking at O'Clery, "My English is pretty good. I heard what your bartender said and understood him just fine. Maybe you don't get what I'm saying. Put a beer and a shot on the bar, and I'll give you four bits. Easy enough."

O'Clery put a hand on North's shoulder. North reached up, grabbed the arm that hand was attached to, and twisted it until O'Clery's head was on the bar. North looked into surprised eyes, "I didn't come for a fight; I came for a drink. But, we can play it your way." He released O'Clery's arm.

O'Clery rubbed his shoulder for a moment and began to turn. Instead of walking away, he spun and took a swing at North, who leaned back on the barstool and evaded the blow. North stood and swung, making contact with the Irishman's midsection. The impact pushed up on O'Clery's diaphragm knocking the air out of his lungs and him to the floor.

A couple of men stood and walked toward North, who pulled his jacket back, revealed both the badge on his belt and the .38 hanging under his arm, "I'm thinking that this isn't a fight you want to be part of."

"Shit, he's a cop," one of the pair said to the other. They backed off and returned to their table. North straightened the Stetson on his head and walked toward the door. A working girl who'd been sitting at the other end of the bar followed him out.

"They play that game when they think they've got a pigeon. You're the first person to call 'em on it."

North pulled a Pall Mall from his pocket. The prostitute extended a hand; he gave her a cigarette and lit it before lighting his own, "And what game are you playing?"

"Me?" She smiled flirtatiously, "I'm wondering if you need a little company for the night."

"You know that I'm a cop, right?"

123

"I saw a badge. Also saw that it isn't from Davenport. But even cops need a little company, don't they?"

North gave her the once over. She probably wasn't that much older than the girls whose murders he was investigating, "Why don't you go home?"

"Please. I need to turn a trick tonight, or I'm going to be in trouble. Don't you find me attractive?"

"How much?"

She was startled by his quick turnaround, "Five dollars for regular sex, or I can do your knob for two."

North pulled two fives out of his wallet, "One's for your pimp, the other's for you."

"For nothing?" she asked.

"For nothing."

"You sure you don't want me to go with you? Just for someone to talk to?" Her question had the sound of desperation.

He walked her up the street toward the hotel, "Where's your pimp?"

"He's in the alley across the street from the bar. He waits there in his car."

"I'm going to ask you a serious question, and I want a straight answer."

She was hesitant, "Okay, I guess."

"Did you run away from home? Is that why you're working the streets?

"Yes," there was sadness in her voice.

"Why don't we walk to my hotel and see if we can't find a way to help you out of this situation?"

"I don't understand. Why would you help me? You don't even know me."

"Let's just say that I wasn't around to help a couple of other girls about your age that got in trouble a long way from home." They continued to walk the half dozen blocks back to the Mississippi Hotel. North was confident there was a car following in the darkness behind them.

He hurried her into an elevator. "Do you want to go home?" he asked as the doors slid shut behind them.

"I can't," she cried.

"Why not?"

"I owe Finnegan money for my food and rent. I've got to work it off before I go."

"Finnegans your pimp?"

She nodded.

"Does Finnegan know where your family lives?"

"He knows I'm from Illinois. He didn't much care where I was from," she said as North turned the key to his door and opened it for her.

"Okay. Illinois covers a lot of ground, so he doesn't know much." North grabbed the telephone directory from the nightstand and flipped to the Vs. He ran his finger down a page before he picked up the receiver.

"Operator."

"This is Mr. North in four-seventeen. Connect me with 2-9837."

"Please hold while I connect your call." The phone connected to that number rang five times before it was answered.

"Hello?"

"Vogel, it's North. I need you to come to the Hotel. I'm in room four-seventeen. And step on it." He paused as Vogel began a stream of questions, "I'll tell you when you get here."

North motioned for the teenager to sit, "My name is Rick North. What's your name?"

"Mary, Mary Dahl." Under the harsh light from the table lamp, she looked every bit the child she was.

"Well, Mary, the man I just spoke with works missing persons here in Davenport. He and I are going to get you back home." He paused long enough to light another cigarette, "I guess I should ask why you left to begin with."

"I had a stupid fight with my mom." Mary began to cry, "I told her I was big enough that I didn't need her telling me what to do and that I could take care of myself."

"Have you spoken with her since you left?"

She shook her head, "She's not going to want me back after what I've done."

"What you've done is proven that you couldn't take care of yourself. Go home and tell her that you were wrong."

"Like the Prodigal Son begged his dad to forgive him?"

North, not having any idea what she was talking about, nodded his head in agreement, "Right." He looked at the bourbon and decided against any until the girl was gone. "Why don't you use the washroom and clean up. I bet there's a pretty girl under all that makeup."

There was a knock on the door while Mary was still in the bath.

126

North pulled the Colt from its holster and called through the door, "Who is it?"

"Vogel. Open the damn door!" North pulled the door open and lowered the gun. "What the Sam Hill is going on?"

"There's a runaway in the bathroom by the name of Mary Dahl. She's been working the streets and needs help getting home."

"What the hell!" Vogel shouted before lowering his voice to a whisper, "Do I look like the Salvation Army?"

About that time, Mary stepped out of the bathroom. Without the heels and makeup, she looked small, young, and fragile.

"Mary, this is Joe. He and I are going to figure out how to get you home." North looked at Vogel, "Right, Joe?"

Vogel scratched the back of his head, "Okay, Mary, where you from?"

Mary sat on the chair she had used earlier, "Rockford, Illinois."

North turned to Vogel, "How far is that?"

"Maybe a hundred twenty miles or so."

Picking up the phone, North called the Operator again. "Connect me with the Greyhound depot. Yeah, I'll wait," he lit a cigarette; the room was quiet. "When does the next bus leave for Rockford, Illinois? Is there room on the bus? Great. Thanks."

"There's a bus that leaves from here for Chicago in two hours, and they stop in Rockford." North turned to Mary, "Do you want to call your mother?"

A tear rolled down the young woman's face, "I'm scared."

Vogel lowered himself to a knee and looked into her eyes, "What are you scared of?" North thought how much more compassionate Vogel was than he was himself.

"I'm afraid she won't want me to come home," she said through a sob.

"We can cross that bridge if we get to it." Vogel put a hand on her shoulder, "Would you like me to talk to your mother first?"

Mary nodded.

"What's her telephone number?" Vogel wrote it down as Mary called out the digits. He picked up the phone, asked the operator to call the number she had given, and hung up the receiver. "They'll call us back when they connect." He lit a cigarette and sat on the edge of the bed. "How long you been here, Mary?"

"It was September." she furrowed her brow for a moment and looked at North and Vogel, "It hasn't even been four months, but it seems like years."

The phone rang; Vogel picked it up. He cupped his hand over the receiver, "What's your mom's name?"

"Uh, Nancy Dahl."

"Hello, Mrs. Dahl? This is Sergeant Joseph Vogel with the Davenport Police Department. Yes... Yes, ma'am..., yes this is about your daughter Mary..., No..., please, Mrs. Dahl. No, she's okay. Yes, she's right here. Would you like to speak with her? Hold on one moment," Vogel put his hand over the mouthpiece, "She sounds anxious to hear your voice."

Mary took the receiver with a shaky hand, "Mama? Oh, Mama. I'm so sorry." Their conversation lasted a few minutes. Finally, Mary ended the call telling her mother that she would be coming in on the bus.

"I can't go!" She cried after she had hung up the phone.

North was confused, "Why's that?"

"I can't wear these clothes home. I look like what I am."

128

Vogel smiled, "My daughter is away at college. I bet we have a closet full of clothes that'll fit you. We'll get you into something warm and a coat and have you on the bus tonight."

Pulling his wallet out, North looked at Vogel. What do you suppose that bus ticket is going to cost?"

"I don't know. Maybe a five-spot."

North grabbed two twenties and handed them to Mary, "This, and the ten I gave you earlier should get you home and give you a little to get what you need when you get there."

She held the bills in her hand for a moment before handing North all but twenty dollars back, "Everything I need is waiting for me at home."

"Joe, you may want to pull around back and take her down the service elevator. Her former pimp may be milling around out front waiting for her to finish with me."

"Good idea." Vogel was back within five minutes. He covered Mary's shoulders with his overcoat. She reached up and gave North a hug, "I don't know how I can ever thank you."

"Just have a good life." North turned to Vogel, "Thank you, Joe."

Joe reached out and shook North's hand, "My dad used to say that you can't shack up with the Devil and expect God to pay the rent. But damn, if you didn't."

Chapter 13

The plane touched down at Lakeland within five minutes of its ETA. North ducked as he exited the aluminum tube that had brought him back from Midway in Chicago. He handed his claim ticket to the baggage handler and was given his bag. As promised, Suzette was there, waiting for him between the plane and the terminal. If anything, she looked better than he had ever seen her.

"Productive trip, detective?" she purred in her breathy voice.

North nodded, "Yeah, doll. Got a few things that are beginning to line up."

"I'm happy to hear that." She grabbed his arm and leaned her head against his arm as they walked. He remembered a night the previous summer when they had walked like this as he took her for an ice cream cone, stopping to look into shop windows as they walked. Her proximity felt good and right.

"It's a little early for dinner," he said as they walked into the hallway that led to her office. "Do you want to grab a drink?"

She pulled him into her office and pushed the door shut with her foot. Away from prying eyes, she reached up, wrapped her arms around North's neck, and kissed him. The kiss was hard, but her lips were incredibly soft. "I've wanted to do that for months," she sighed.

North stepped back to look at her—Suzette Arquette was the image of his ideal woman; tall, buxom, and confident. But there was something more about Suzette. North looked into her eyes as he held her face between his hands; she was a puzzle. A gorgeous woman who had shot a mobster to save his life and seemed unbothered by having done so. A woman doing a man's job as an airport manager but, at the same time, soft and vulnerable. North leaned down and kissed her again, "And I've wanted to do that since the moment I met you."

"And you didn't because you were seeing," she paused. "I'm sorry, I don't even know her name."

"Sylvia. Her name was Sylvia."

"I have a very real idea of how much she meant to you, and I'm not looking to replace her. But, like I told you last summer on the bluff, I feel about you the way you felt about her."

The words hung in the air for a moment as North pushed a wave of guilt back where it belonged. "Where do you want to go for a drink?"

"I thought you might want to take me to the Navajo," the brunette said, referring to an upscale restaurant a dozen miles south of LaSalle Harbor.

"Oh, you did, did you?" North chuckled as he lit a cigarette.

Suzette smiled, "the owner flew out of here for Christmas. He handed me his card and told me that he would give me a complimentary dinner for two."

North looked at the business card, *The Navajo, Fine Dining and Cocktails, U.S. 12, Bridgman, Michigan. Dominic D'Agostino, Owner/Chef.* The back of the card bore D'Agostino's signature and a note granting the bearer two free dinners. "Well, who am I to turn down a free meal?" he looked at Suzette, "Hope you don't mind going in my old pickup."

She thought about it for a moment before she reached for her purse, "Why don't we take my car? It might be more comfortable than your truck."

He shrugged and followed her outside to a red-over-white Plymouth Savoy. "Nice. Do you want me to drive?" he reached toward the keys.

Suzette pulled the keys away from his reach, "I think you might find that I'm more than competent behind the wheel." She unlocked the passenger door for North before walking around and letting herself into the driver's door. He smiled at her independence. The flathead six fired up as soon as the key was turned. She turned and looked over her shoulder as she backed out of her parking spot. He admired her high cheekbones and the soft lips that he had just kissed. Then, pulling the gearshift into drive, the car hurtled out of the lot at Lakeland Airport and down Territorial Road toward town.

North smiled as he lit a Pall Mall, "You drive like you've got somewhere to go."

Her laugh was playful, lilting, and utterly captivating, "I've been told that I drive like I've got a trunkful of moonshine. I haven't seen you in six months; catch me up."

North wasn't sure the car had actually touched the bridge as they flew over it, crossing the river. As the Plymouth rocketed toward the restaurant, North told her about the corruption at the local and state levels that had caused him to be put on leave and his time in Hell. They sat in the restaurant's parking lot for a while as he spoke about Sylvia's visit and her sudden death.

"Sylvia must have been something," Suzette finally said as she watched Brick stare off into the distance. "Tell me about her."

He gave her a doubtful look, "I think it's better if we just leave it."

"I want to know about her because it'll tell me something about you. What made her attractive?"

North lit a cigarette and thought. "She was small and vulnerable,"

"And you were the white knight who was going to protect her?"

"I guess that was part of it."

"And what makes me attractive?"

He looked across the seat as the headlights of a car swept through the Plymouth and silhouetted her figure, "Other than your conspicuous assets," he took a drag on the Pall Mall, "It feels like you're my equal. You're strong and tough. You stand up for yourself and aren't afraid to ask for what you want."

She gave a gentle laugh and put her hand on North's arm, "It's funny you say that. You're the first man who treats me like an equal. I don't sense that you have a need to feel superior."

Once inside the restaurant, they were guided to a table in the center of the room. North looked at the hostess and pointed to a table in the corner, "We'll take that one." Once there, he held the chair for Suzette and sat with the wall against his back. Native rugs hung against the knotty pine paneling around the dining room. These absorbed massive amounts of sound. Even though there were dozens of diners, it was easy to imagine they were by themselves.

North sipped at his bourbon as he looked across the table at Suzette. Her forest green velvet dress was the perfect foil to her alabaster skin and brunette hair. He looked at the gimlet she had ordered. "What, exactly, is that?" he asked.

"A gimlet is gin and sweetened lime juice. It's Philip Marlowe's favorite drink. Would you like to try a sip?"

Lighting a cigarette, North gave Suzette a curious look, "Philip who?"

She laughed infectiously, "Philip Marlow, the detective in the Raymond Chandler books."

"Never heard of him," he took a drag on a Pall Mall.

"Don't you read?"

"If I were to read, it wouldn't be a detective story."

"Why's that?"

"Because they always get everything wrong."

"Oh, really," she giggled. "And you always get everything right?"

North smiled, something he rarely did. It was a big, toothy grin. He looked across the table, "Actually, I get things wrong all the time. Detectives in the movies and in books always get everything right all the time, which is why they're wrong."

Suzette shook her head as she reached for North's cigarette; it was handed back with red lipstick on the white paper, "They're wrong because they're right?"

Grinning, North nodded, "That made a lot more sense when I said it." They both laughed.

In the parking lot after dinner, Suzette handed North the keys. He gave her an inquiring look, "You want me to drive this race car of yours?"

"If you drive, I can sit next to you. If I drive, you'll sit next to the door, and I really want to be next to you."

North turned the ignition key and put the gear lever into reverse, "I'll take you back to the airport and get my truck."

Suzette, sitting in the middle of the bench seat, squeezed his arm, "Is our date over so soon?"

"It doesn't need to be. Where did you want to go?"

"I want to see this house you bought," she leaned her head on his shoulder and looked up at him.

Saturday morning dawned cold and clear. A steady wind blew over the open waters of Lake Michigan and pounded against the front of the little house on Vine Street. North yawned and sat on the edge of the bed for a minute before pushing himself onto his feet. He was pleasantly surprised that it was the first night in a long time that he had not been awakened by memories of the war. After using the bathroom, he got the percolator going on the stove.

"That smells good," Suzette said as she stepped out of the bedroom wearing the robe and slippers from the bag she had stashed in the trunk of her car. She walked over and hugged North, "Thank you for last night."

"You took care of dinner. I only bought a couple of drinks."

She playfully slapped him on the arm, "You know what I meant."

"Thank you, too." He kissed her on the forehead.

"What's for breakfast in this hashhouse you're running?"

North shrugged, "Well, if I'm perfectly honest, not much."

Suzette pushed him aside and looked through the icebox and cabinets. Opening her purse, she pulled out a pen and a piece of paper and began writing.

"What are you up to?" North asked from across the kitchen.

"Making you a shopping list. Now go get dressed; you're going to the market."

"I am?" he asked teasingly.

She pointed toward the bedroom, "Last night, you said that I wasn't afraid to ask for what I want. I'm asking. Now go get some clothes on."

He appeared a few minutes later in dungarees and a flannel shirt. Suzette smiled at him, "I've never seen you in casual clothes. You look good." She stopped him as he was pulling the old Mackinaw on, "Didn't anyone ever tell you that you can't wear multiple plaids at once?"

"No, why?" North reached for the keys to his pickup, "Crap, my truck is still at the airport."

Suzette tossed him her keys, "Don't break my car!"

Grinning, North tipped the Stetson and walked out the back door.

Damaske's was busy for nine o'clock on a Saturday morning. He ran down Suzette's list, putting each item in the basket he carried. Looking at the list and thinking aloud, "Okay, a quart of milk, a can of orange juice, a loaf of bread, butter, and eggs. All I need is bacon." He made his way to the butcher's counter at the back of the store.

"What'll it be?" the butcher asked.

"Fix me up with a pound of bacon." North reexamined the list making sure that he hadn't forgotten anything.

"Hey, your that detective we talked to before Christmas," the butcher said as he placed the white tape onto the paper wrapped around the bacon.'

"Yeah, that's me."

"West, isn't it?" the butcher handed the bacon across the counter.

"North."

"Well, our sausage casing friend was back. He was here when we opened at eight. Picked up another hank of casings."

"He was here less than a week ago, and now he needs another three hundred feet of the stuff?"

"And, get this. He wants me to order enough that he can come in once a week and get more."

"Did he say when he'll be back?" North pushed the bacon into the handbasket.

"Told me that he'll be in next Saturday morning."

North pushed the Stetson back on his head, "You didn't happen to get his name, did you?"

"I tried. Told him that I liked to get to know my customers, but he wasn't very cooperative."

"Any chance you got anything on the car?"

The butcher shook his head, "I followed him to the front of the store, but he must have been parked around the corner. Didn't see a car."

North thought quietly before leaning slightly over the counter and spoke in hushed tones with the butcher. The butcher nodded his head in agreement. North's plan in place, he took the groceries home to a shapely brunette who apparently could cook.

Chapter 14

Like most days in early Winter, North's day began in the dark; even the moon provided no illumination as it would be midday before it would rise. He had finished breakfast at the Fifth Wheel and was at his desk before the sun rose at quarter past eight. Tiffin arrived on North's heels, "Welcome back; did you have a quiet weekend?"

North shook his head and smiled, "As quiet as a church mouse's."

"There's a mixed metaphor in there somewhere," Tiffin laughed as he hung up his coat and hat.

"How's that?" North lit a Pall Mall.

"You shook your head no and answered in the affirmative. So, did you have a quiet weekend or not?"

"Can we just say that I had a good weekend and leave it at that?" North picked a piece of loose tobacco off his lip, rolled it between his fingers, and flicked it onto the linoleum.

"Well, if that's how you going to play it…," Tiffin poured a cup of coffee from the urn and shook powdered creamer into his cup. "By the way, the chief gave us four men to go door-to-door on Saturday morning."

North leaned forward on his chair, "They come up with anything?"

"No one acknowledged knowing your Doctor Doolen if that's what you mean."

"So, a cop knocks on your door and asks if you know a Doctor Doolen. How easy is it to just say no? I'm pretty sure the Fuller Brush man wouldn't take no as quickly as our officers did."

"You're probably right. They could have spoken to Doolen and not have known it."

"Without a picture to go on, we're dead in the water."

"Oh, speaking of pictures, we got the dental records Vogel sent for his missing girls. Doc Howard says that they were an exact match for the remains he has at the Morgue."

"I was pretty sure they were going to be," North took a pull on his cigarette, held the smoke for a moment before blowing it toward the ceiling. "So, we know who they were. Where they went missing from and when. But we don't know how they got here or how they died."

Tiffin sipped on his coffee, "You think that Doolen brought a girl with him once a year from Iowa to LaSalle Harbor. He did that from fifty-three to fifty-five, and then he stopped. Why? Why did he stop bringing girls here?"

North thought for a moment, "Perhaps Doolen stopped coming to Michigan for a while, or he found girls here to fill his needs, whatever those might be. Or, he no longer had the need."

"If he took girls from here, we'd have missing girls. Yet, we've come up with nothing searching Missing Persons in the tri-state area."

"Okay, scratch that," North took another pull on the Pall Mall. "That leaves us with he either stopped coming to Michigan, or he no longer needed the girls."

"The blood type thing rules out sexual perversion, right?"

"I don't know that we can rule anything out."

"So, what's our next move?"

"At nine, we head over to the Registrar of Deeds office and see if we can come up with anything on Doolen."

North deftly parallel-parked the Mainline in front of the three-story limestone courthouse that had been in use since the late nineteenth century. He and Tiffin made their way to the second-floor office of the Douglas County Register of Deeds. The counter was staffed by the same twenty-something-year-old blonde they had encountered on their visit in July. She smiled as the detectives entered the office, "I remember you two. You looking for a guy with an Italian name again?"

"No," North smiled, "this time, we're looking for property owned by someone with an Irish name."

She grinned, "Oh sure, that'll narrow it down. What area of the county do you want to look?"

"Off Lake Bluff Park and maybe on the beach."

"Okay, that's only one book. What's the name?"

North spelled out Doolen. After having checked every property along the bluff and beach, they began searching further inland. Finally, after forty-five minutes of futile hunting, they left.

"That was fruitless," Tiffin said as they stepped outside.

North lit a cigarette, "Well, we've ruled out being able to take the easy road."

"There's never an easy road."

"You've noticed that too, have you?" North chuckled.

"So, where to next?"

Back in the Ford, North flipped through his old leather notepad, "What say we wander back to the UnderTow?"

Looking confused, Tiffin lit a smoke, "We've got the Baxter guy who can testify to what old Machine Gun said about being with Cudlip the night of the murder. What else are you looking at?"

"You remember the waitress, Dolly?"

Tiffin thought for a moment before he nodded, "Yeah, Chapman, Dolly Chapman. So?"

"I've got this gut feeling that she knows more than she let on last time we were there." North turned the car toward the river and the docks. Within five minutes, they were parked in the dirt lot next to the run-down building that housed the bar.

At ten o'clock in the morning, Tiffin was surprised to find a few patrons were already sipping cheap beer. The bartender looked up as the detectives walked in. The detectives flashed their badges. "What can I do for you dicks?" the bartender asked with an edge to his voice.

North lit a cigarette and paused to draw in a lung full of smoke before he spoke, "You can tell me where I can find Dolly Chapman."

The bartender looked around the bar, "I don't see Dolly."

"Did you catch that, Tiff? The guy thinks he's a comedian."

Tiffin looked into the bartender's eyes, "He's no Milton Berle."

North leaned across the bar, grabbed the front of the bartender's shirt, and pulled him forward, "I'm only going to ask this one more time. Where can I find Dolly Chapman?"

"How the hell should I know?"

One of the men nursing a beer looked over, "She's your old lady; you ought to know where she is." The other men in the bar laughed.

North released his grip on the shirt, "Your old lady. Where is she, Mr. Chapman?"

"I'm not Chapman. We ain't married. We just, you know, share a space."

North grinned, "Hey partner, you remember your penal code?"

"Which part?" Tiffin cocked his head.

"Act three twenty-eight of the 1931 code," North took a drag on the cigarette that had glued itself to the corner of his lip.

The bartender looked between the two detectives, "What are you yapping about?"

"Act three twenty-eight, section 335 refers to lascivious cohabitation and gross lewdness."

"What the fuck are you talking about?!"

Tiffin, after recalling the specific act, quoted from memory, "Any man or woman, not being married to each other, who lewdly and lasciviously associates and cohabits together, is guilty of a misdemeanor punishable by imprisonment for not more than one year, or a fine of not more than one thousand dollars."

The bartender was defensive and confused, "I don't know what the fuck you're talking about."

North looked at Tiffin, "Tell him what we're talking about."

"We're telling you that here in Michigan, it's against the law to shack up with your old lady."

"Now," North began, "either turn around so I can handcuff you or tell me where Dolly is."

"You've got to be fucking kidding me!" the bartender shouted. There ain't no law against me and Dolly living together."

142

"Your lawyer can probably explain it to you better than I can." Turning to his partner, North added, "Cuff him and take him to the car."

"Alright, alright," the bartender pleaded, "She's upstairs in the apartment. Dolly probably ain't even up yet. Let me go up and wake her."

North took him by the arm, "We'll all go up together."

The three of them walked through a curtained doorway at the back of the barroom and into a cramped storage room. A steep staircase was located in the corner. North led them up the stairs, with Tiffin following the bartender. The door was unlocked, and North pushed it open; the dry hinges squealed as the door swung inward. Once inside the small dirty apartment, North swept his eyes around and walked to the only area that could be a bedroom. Dolly Chapman was stretched out on the bed under a comforter stitched together from old clothes.

"I thought you lived with your aunt, Miss Chapman," North shouted.

Startled, Dolly sat up and instinctively pulled the comforter up to cover her nakedness. "Chet? What are they doing in here?"

The bartender looked down, "I'm sorry, Dolly. They kind of have the upper hand."

"I don't think you were honest with us last Thursday when we picked up Bobby Baxter."

The barmaid looked between her boyfriend and the detectives, "I told you that I didn't hear anything."

Tiffin looked at his notes and shook his head, "No. Last week you said you didn't see anything. Now you're telling us you didn't hear anything. Which is it?"

"See anything, hear anything, what's the difference?"

"The difference is it sounds like you're lying to us." North lit a cigarette, "And we don't like to be lied to."

143

"If you don't cooperate, we will take you in for violation of the lewd and lascivious cohabitation act." Tiffin pushed his hat to the back of his head. Miss Chapman just stared at him.

"That means it's against the law for us to shack up," Chet volunteered.

"It means that if you cooperate, we might forget we found you in violation of the law," North blew smoke toward the low ceiling.

"I don't want trouble, especially from the likes of Machine Gun," a tear rolled down Dolly's cheek.

Chet looked an imploring look, "Dolly, a year in jail and a fine of a grand."

"Each," North added.

"Each," Chet repeated.

"Okay. Yeah, I overheard Machine Gun talking to Baxter. He said that some guy with a cut lip owed him a few bucks, and they fought. The guy with the cut lip got hit in the head with a brick, and Machine Gun dug through the guys' pockets and came up with forty cents."

North scratched a few notes, "Think. Did Kelly say that he hit the man with a brick?"

"Yeah, maybe."

"No maybes. Yes or no. Did Kelly tell Baxter that he hit the man with a brick?"

"Yes," she cried, "Yes, he said that he hit the man with a brick."

"You will be called as a witness, and you will testify. Or, I will charge you with the crime you are guilty of." North looked at his notes, "You have an aunt that lives on McAlister?"

"Yes, my Aunt Mildred."

"What's the street address?"

"Five forty-seven McAlister."

North consulted his notes and verified it was the same address that she had given previously. "What's Mildred's last name?"

"Hull. My aunt's name is Mildred Hull."

"Okay, Dolly, that's where the court will send the subpoena and where you better be living, or I will come back and lock you both up." North pushed the Stetson onto his mop of hair and led Tiffin out of the apartment.

Outside, Tiffin looked at North, "No one has been arrested for shaking up in years."

"I know that," North smiled, "but they don't."

Chapter 15

Chief Cummings looked across his desk at North as he tamped moist tobacco into the bowl of his pipe, "I've got to admit, you made some headway going to Iowa. How much did that trip set you back?"

North picked a piece of loose tobacco off his lip, "With the plane ticket, hotel, and meals, about two hundred. But, that includes helping a runaway get back home to her mother."

The chief shook his head, "I wish I could reimburse you for that, but I don't have those kinds of funds available."

"Yeah, don't worry about it. I needed to go."

Cummings sucked the flame from a match into the bowl of the pipe, "Okay, catch me up of the case against Kelly George."

"I've got two witnesses that overheard George discussing Cudlip's death. One of them heard him say George struck Cudlip with a brick before digging through his pockets."

"You get a confession from George?" a fragrant plume of smoke rose from the pipe.

"He hasn't said two words since his arrest."

"You've got a pretty weak case against him." The chief paused to tamp the tobacco down, "Where are you on locating this Doolen?"

"The county doesn't have any record of a Doolen owning any property near Lake Bluff Park or on the lakefront."

Cumming's frustration was evident, "Why was your search so limited?"

North lit a Pall Mall, "A hunch based upon where the bodies were located."

"I don't care if you have to look at every property in the county. I want you to find this character. Have you checked with the Tax Assessors' Office?"

North didn't like to be questioned, even by his boss, "I'm positive we're going to find the good Doctor in my search area. But, we'll go back and continue to go through the property records."

"And don't forget to look at property tax records." Cummings relit his pipe, "No one can just disappear. He's got to bank somewhere, doesn't he? So check the banks while you're out there."

"Okay, Chief!" North turned toward the door, "We're on it."

Cummings called out as North walked into the squad room, "Drycleaners, mechanics, watchmakers, dentists, anywhere a man might need to go and leave his name!"

 Tiffin looked up at North as he walked across the room, "Okay, partner, where to first?"

"The Trophy Room sounds good about now," North grabbed his Stetson and headed for the stairs.

"Hey, Brick, wait up!" Tiffin shouted as he pulled on his overcoat.

Over lunch, the detectives laid out their game plan. Tiffin would work with the Assessor's Office while North would see if he could talk the young blonde at the Registrar's Office into digging through her plat books. The two sat in silence while Tiffin finished his burger, and North sipped his second shot.

"Oh!" Tiffin looked across the table. "I almost forgot. Kaye wants you to come over tomorrow night."

"It's Tuesday night. Why would you want me over?"

Tiffin shook his head, "It's New Year's Eve! We're having a couple of friends over to say good riddance to fifty-seven and to welcome in fifty-eight."

North played with the empty shot glass, "One of those friends wouldn't happen to be a single woman that your wife knows, would it?"

Shrugging, Tiffin wiped his mouth with a paper napkin, "I really don't know who she's invited."

"But…"

"But, it wouldn't surprise me. Kaye sees herself as a bit of a *Shadchanit.*"

"A who?" North held his glass up, signaling for another shot.

"A matchmaker. Every Jewish wife wants to make sure that every other woman is as happy as she is."

Roxy, having overheard Tiffin's last comment, laughed, "Or as miserable as she is." She sat the shot of whiskey in front of North, collected the empty glass, and walked back to the bar.

"Thank Kaye for me. But I'll be staying home."

"So, what are you going to do with your New Year's Eve?"

"I don't have any plans other than to avoid the amateur drinkers who get juiced-up and try to drive home," North tossed back the third shot of whiskey, that along with a beer, had been his lunch.

"Not professional drinkers like yourself."

"Exactly." North crushed out the cigarette he'd been smoking, "You ready to find Doolen?"

Tiffin rose and pulled on his overcoat while North put his suit jacket over the worn leather holster that hung over his shoulders. "You know, between the Cutlip murder and chasing this Dr. Doolen, it feels like we've been chasing ghosts."

North paused as he began to push the Stetson onto his head. "Sometimes it feels like the ghosts are chasing me," he said in a low voice.

"How's that?"

Sitting back down at the table, North began to tell Tiffin about his history of vivid nightmares that had followed him since the war. "Most of the dreams take place in this little church in Freyneux, France, during the Battle of the Bulge. The scene is always the same, but the person I'm with is different."

Tiffin listened intently, "Different, how?"

"Sometimes, it's the soldier that I had met up with. He was…" North paused as he took a drag on his cigarette, "…killed there. But, recently, Sylvia has been in the dream. She's always crying and asking where I am."

"Damn, Brick. Why haven't you ever told me about this?"

"Because I think I'm going crazy, and that's not something you wander around telling people."

"What if I tell you that there are times I feel like I'm still on the New Mexico right after we were hit by kamikazes in the shelling of Lingayen Gulf? I was aft of the explosion below decks. I was lucky. I escaped with only minor injuries; so many of my mates died that day or in the following days. A dozen years later, and there are times that I can hear the explosions and the men screaming. I can feel the heat of the fires

149

scorching my skin. Sometimes I wake up screaming. Kaye's a trooper to put up with me."

"Geez, Barry, I didn't know. I'm glad you made it home."

Tiffin looked down, "That's the hitch, and I know it sounds stupid, but why did I live and so many others didn't?"

"I talked to a bartender when I was in Hell. He told me that lots of us, how did he put it? Oh yeah," North pointed at his head. "Lots of us have scars that aren't visible."

Tiffin reached across the table and shook North's hand, "I think there are more of us with those kinds of scars than not. And we're all afraid of admitting we have problems."

North paused to light a cigarette, "This is going to sound crazy, but I think that in some ways, these nightmares have helped make me who I am. That I'm stronger because I've had to fight through them."

"It's not crazy. On the contrary, the war shaped each of us into who we are."

Looking at his watch, North stood, "We need to get back to the Court House."

"We need to continue this talk," Tiffin said as he stood.

"What? Is this going to become some AA-type meeting for guys who were in the war?" North dropped three dollars on the bar for their two dollar and thirty-five cent bill, "Keep the change, Rox," he said as he pulled the door open.

"Thanks, Brick. See you tomorrow," the big old friendly gal called after him.

Back at the Safety Building, Tiffin checked the car out from the Motor Pool. Within minutes they were parked outside the courthouse, "Okay, I'm heading to the Assessor's Office. I'll probably be done before you are."

North nodded, "Come find me when you're done."

The young blonde that worked in the Registrar of Deeds Office smiled When North entered the office, "Missed me already, did you?"

"Exactly, doll. I couldn't wait to spend more time with you." North leaned on the counter and looked into the clerk's hazel eyes, "That and my boss wants me to look further afield."

"Did you leave your friend behind so we could be alone?" the clerk cooed as she leaned in.

North grinned, "Guilty as charged. So where do we begin?"

"Dinner would be nice."

"I meant with finding if a Gerald Doolen owns property in the area."

"You know what they say about all work and no play," she called over her shoulder as she walked between two shelving units. She came back a minute later with two large plat books, "You look through the one that covers from the river to the southern city limit, I'll look through from the river to the northern limit."

Tiffin joined North within twenty minutes of having gone to the Assessors office, "Sorry, Brick, there's no record of a Gerald or any other Doolen who pays property taxes in LaSalle Harbor."

North looked at the blonde clerk, "You have any other plat books my friend can search?"

"We can look at townships outside the city limits." She paused for a moment as she thought, "The question is, which direction do you want to start? South, north, or east of town?"

"Do I get a vote?" Tiffin joked.

Shaking his head, North looked at his partner, "It really doesn't matter. Doolen isn't outside the city. He's close to the Cooper-Wells building, and there's no property registered to him."

151

"But the chief said…," Tiffin began.

"Screw the chief!" North retorted. "The only reason Doolen dumped those bodies at the factory is that it was close."

The clerk looked up in surprise, "Bodies?! You're looking for the man who murdered the Sand Rabbit girls the paper talked about?"

Tiffin lit a cigarette, "Yes, but the girls weren't Sand Rabbits. We traced them to Iowa."

"And this Doolen you're looking for murdered them?" There was shock in the clerk's voice.

"We're just going where the clues lead us." North gave her a stern look and cautioned, "Keep this under your hat."

"Who could I blab this to that would matter?"

North put his hand on her forearm; he felt her tremble at his touch, "You tell someone, who tells someone, who mentions it to another that maybe knows Doolen, and he bolts before we can catch up with him."

"Okay, I see."

"You've been very helpful, Miss?"

"Christine House. But everyone calls me Chris."

"Thank you, Chris."

"Come back again," she called after them as they left the office.

Tiffin started the Ford and let the car idle, "Okay, what's next?"

"The chief is right about one thing, Doolen is going to need the same basics as the rest of us. Drycleaning is a good place to start." There were a dozen dry cleaners in town; they started at Barlow's and worked their way from cleaners to cleaners. By three o'clock, they stopped at the last dry cleaner on their list, Aristo Cleaners. North picked up his own clothes as he talked to the owner, "Charlie, I'm looking for a guy by the name of Doolen, Gerald Doolen. You do any work for him?"

"Name's familiar. Let me ask the missus." He looked past the racks of clothes, "Iota? You take any work for a guy by the name of Doolen?"

Mrs. Kizer came to the front counter, "Doolen, you say?"

"That's right," North agreed. "Gerald Doolen. Retired guy, so probably in his sixties."

She flipped through the yellow tickets on the spindle next to the cash drawer. Finally, near the bottom of the stack, she found what she was looking for, "Jerry Doolen. He picked up a three-piece suit, a sports coat, and some slacks first thing this morning."

North flipped his worn leather notepad open, "Did he leave an address or a phone number with you?"

"No, just his name."

"He didn't happen to pay you with a check, did he?"

"I don't think so, but let me look." She went through the handful of checks in the cash drawer, "No, it must have been cash."

North tipped his hat, "Thank you. You've both been very helpful."

Charlie smiled, "Glad to help. See you next time." The bell over the front door tinkled as North walked outside. He threw his cleaning on the backseat of the Mainline and climbed into the passenger seat.

"Find anything other than your clothes?" Tiffin asked.

"He was here just this morning."

"These folks know where to find him?"

"Not a clue, Tiff. Not a clue."

"Damn, Doolen must be known to someone in town," Tiffin's voice revealed his frustration.

"If he's using Aristo Cleaners, he might be visiting other shops nearby. So let's walk the neighborhood."

As dusk fell, they had visited every newsstand, candy store, shoe repair, drug store, and food market within a two-block radius of the cleaners. It was a long shot as most businesses were cash-and-carry. Back in the car, North tossed his hat onto the seat and ran his hand through his hair, "Dammit, Tiff, someone has to know Doolen and where he lives."

Tiffin shook his head, "We're both stupid! If he's walking around with money in his pocket, he's got to bank somewhere."

"And there's only a handful of banks in town!" North flipped the lid to his Zippo open and lit a cigarette, "They're all closed for the day; we'll visit them first thing in the morning."

Gatto was waiting at the backdoor for North when he pulled into the drive. The cat was keeping the two Wolfe boys occupied. "What are you boys up to?" North asked as he stepped out of the pickup.

The older of the boys spoke up, "Mama has made a sauerbraten and wants to know if you would like to eat with us?" The boys were visibly excited; North didn't know if it was because roast beef was on the menu or because they wanted him to eat with them.

He paused for a moment before answering. "What time would your mother like me there?"

The younger Wolfe boy spoke up, "Mama says supper is at seven."

Chapter 16

The Wolfe house was just a block west from North's place. After feeding Gatto and having liberated a fair amount of bourbon from its bottle, North walked over. His knock on the front door was met with the boys shouting, "He's here, mama."

He removed his hat as she pulled the door open, "Mr. North," she said in her heavily-accented English, "please to come into our home." Without the heavy cloth coat and scarf, Adele Wolfe was more attractive than North had imagined. Her brown hair was naturally curly and worn loose around her shoulders, and the brown of her eyes was so deep it was difficult to distinguish the pupil from the iris.

"It's hard to turn down an invitation when your door is blocked by two boys talking about sauerbraten."

Adele smiled modestly, "Mr. Damaske offered me a piece of beef that was how do you say, *aus der Prime gehen*?"

"Needing to be sold quickly?" North offered.

"Yes, that is it, aged too long, which is perfect for sauerbraten. So the boys and I thought that maybe you would like a hearty meal. Her sons stood near the kitchen entrance smiling.

"Have my sons introduced themselves to you? Do you their names know?"

North shook his head, "No. I only know them as your sons."

Turning to the boys, she whispered in German, "*Sei höflich und stell dich vor*," be polite and introduce yourselves.

The eldest boy stepped forward and gave a deep bow, "I am Jack; I was named for my father."

The younger son stayed near the kitchen but also bowed, "I am Ernst; I am named for my *Opa*."

Adele looked up at North, "He was named after my father."

North acknowledged them with a nod of his head in each boy's direction.

"I do not have anything for you to drink but coffee. Is that good?"

"Coffee is fine, thank you."

Jack came and sat next to North in the living room as his mother went into the kitchen, "So, do you shoot mobsters and stuff?"

"I try not to shoot anyone."

"But, you do get to shoot people, don't you?" The boy sounded disappointed.

"There are times that it's the only thing that a police officer can do, but we would rather not if we can help it."

"But you are not a police officer! You are a detective!" Jack protested. "We got to watch Richard Diamond, Private Detective, on TV at our friend's house. He gets to shoot bad guys."

"And Badge 714!" Ernst added. "Detective Friday shoots bad guys, too!"

North lit a cigarette, "I hate to disappoint you, but real-life detectives spend more time doing paperwork than shooting bad guys."

Adele stepped out of the kitchen with a platter of sauerbraten, rotkohl, and spaetzle. She looked at her sons and snapped, "*Geh hände waschen!*" Then, to North, she said, "Forgive my sons, Mr. North. They are curious about your work."

"They were not bothering me, and please call me Brick."

"Brick? That is an unusual name, yes?"

North grinned, "It's a nickname someone gave me a long time ago."

"Oh! It is your *spitzname*. I understand. But, then, what is the name of your birth?"

"Like Jack, I was named after my father. His name was Brian Richard. My mother called him Brian, and to ease confusion, I was called Rick, which is short for my middle name."

She nodded her head, "Then I will call you Brick, but you must call me Del. Please come to the table." North was directed to the head of the table. The boys returned from the bathroom and sat at the sides. Adele sat at the foot. She looked across the table, "No one has sat there since my husband."

"Would it be better if you and I traded places?"

"No, it is good to have a man at the table again." She looked to her sons, "Please give the grace."

Jack and Ernst's chins dropped to their chests. Adele bowed her head as the boys recited in unison, "Come, Lord Jesus, be our guest, and let thy gifts to us be blessed. Amen."

North said an uncomfortable Amen, a half-beat behind Jack and Ernst. He was exceedingly grateful that he had not been invited to lead the prayer. After an excellent meal, the boys cleared the table and began doing the dishes. He and Adele sat in the living room.

"I hope that I was not too, uh, how do you say, too forwards?"

"Not at all. I am glad that you invited me over. Both for a good dinner and to get to know you."

"I am afraid that men do not find a thirty-year-old woman with two sons to be, uh," she paused to find the right word, "a catch."

"They are sharp boys, and you are a very attractive woman," North lit a cigarette which Adele reached for. She took a drag off the Pall Mall before handing it back to Brick.

"Again, I am too forwards perhaps, but do you think you might see me again?"

North gave her a gentle look, "To be honest, I'm not looking to settle down."

She put her hand on his leg, "Certainly, my sons, they will need a man to help raise them. But right now, I am a woman who is also with needs."

They were interrupted by Ernst running into the room, "Mama, Jack is making me wash and dry the dishes by myself!"

"Excuse me," Adele said as she stood and strode out of the room. He noticed that she looked just as good from the back as she did from the front. North could hear her chastising the boys. He was glancing at his watch when she came back, "Oh, is it so late that you must go?"

"I have an early start tomorrow morning. So, yes, it's time for me to go." Adele leaned forward and kissed him. North was surprised by how gentle and tender the kiss was.

When he leaned back, he saw a tear glide down her cheek. "Forgive me," she said as she wiped the tear away with the back of her hand. "It has been since I lost my husband that I have kissed a man."

North used his thumb to wipe away another tear that began its journey down her cheek. Then, putting two fingers under her chin, he lifted her mouth to his.

In his dream, it was Christmas morning, and North had again sought shelter in the ancient Chapelle du maître. He could hear the Panzer IV tanks rumbling up the road, shaking the ancient church as they came. Within minutes there was pounding on the oaks doors which he had barred. A voice shouted through the doors, *"Herauskommen. Es wird alles in Ordnung sein. Ich werde dich in Sicherheit bringen."* "Come out. It will be okay. I will keep you safe." The voice was Adele Wolfe's.

His nightly walk took him past Adele's house. At two in the morning, not a single light showed through a window. North stood in the street and smoked a cigarette while memories of the dream replayed in his head. After crushing the cigarette under his shoe, he walked past the Cooper-Wells buildings and wandered the boardwalk of the shuttered amusement park. Gatto met him at the door of the house when he returned from his walk.

Tuesday morning dawned overcast but a seasonal twenty-nine degrees. Marie was standing behind the counter with the coffee pot in hand as North entered the Fifth Wheel. "Good morning, detective," she said cheerily as North dropped the Stetson onto the stool next to his. "Anything other than coffee?"

North smiled as he spread the paper on the counter in front of him, "What's the cook pushing today?"

"Oh, you mean what's today's special?"

He took a deep swig of the coffee, "Whatever you want to call it. What do you recommend today?"

The young waitress laughed, "Shredded Wheat pancakes and fried Spam."

"Maybe I'll just have coffee today."

159

She shrugged, "I had one of the pancakes; they're actually pretty good."

"Okay, I'm taking your word for it. Go ahead and bring me an order of it." North turned to the paper while the waitress went to serve a couple of truck drivers. The headline of the LaSalle Palladium read, '57 DEPARTING; EVERYONE GLAD. Immediately under the headline, the lead article was labeled, L.H. COMMISSION DOOMS TIN CITY. "Well, Fuchs is getting fucked," North spoke into the coffee cup.

"What's that?" Marie asked as she walked to the service window.

"Just an old man who is losing his job and his home."

"That's sad."

North shook his head, "It is, and it isn't. Something tells me that Harry is the kind of guy who'll land on his feet."

Having eaten his breakfast with customary enthusiasm, he made eye contact with the waitress who walked to North's regular place at the counter, "Well, whatcha think of Shredded Wheat pancakes?"

"This still the same new cook you had last week?" North wiped his mouth with a paper napkin.

"Yeah, same guy. Why?"

"He needs to stick with steak and eggs. How much do I owe you?"

Marie looked at the ticket, "Forty-five cents."

North took a one-dollar silver certificate from his wallet and laid it on the counter, "Keep the change."

"You ever gonna call me?" Marie asked with a playful edge to her voice.

He pushed his Stetson onto his head and walked to the door where he turned and gave the young waitress the once over. "I just might," he said as he stepped outside.

Tiffin was just coming into the building as North entered, "Kaye wants to know if you're coming tonight."

"What time's this party of hers?" North took the terrazzo stairs to the second floor two at a time.

"Eight o'clock, but you can come earlier if you want," Tiffin raced to catch up.

North tossed his hat onto the coat rack next to his desk, "Eight? Darn," he said sarcastically, "that's past my bedtime. Maybe next year."

"Kaye really wants you to come," Tiffin's voice had a pleading quality to it.

"So she can fix me up with someone she knows? I think I'll take a raincheck."

Tiffin smiled, "Who knows, you might actually like who she has lined up."

"Then again, I might not." North lit a cigarette and began looking through the duty sergeant's reports in the Unit's mailbox.

At nine o'clock, Tiffin called dispatch and let them know that he and North were heading for the Farmers and Merchants Bank on Main. It was a short drive from the Safety Building, and within minutes they were walking into the newly remodeled main floor. At the back of the lobby, the massive round vault door stood open, entry blocked by steel bars. They walked past the teller windows to a wooden railing that blocked a series of wooden desks from the lobby floor. A man looked up from the ledger he was studying, "May I help you, gentlemen?"

North flashed his badge, "I'm Detective North, this is Detective Tiffin."

161

"Good morning, I'm Joseph Mercier; I'm the assistant cashier. How may I help you?"

"Mr. Mercier, we are looking for information on someone who may bank with you," North lit a cigarette and picked a piece of loose tobacco off his lip.

"Who might that be?"

"A Gerald or Jerry Doolen," Tiffin said.

"The name is not familiar, but with thousands of depositors, I can't remember everyone. Give me a moment and let me check our card files." Mercier stood, straightened his suit jacket, and walked over to a row of card files, not unlike the card catalog found in the library. He returned within two minutes. "I'm sorry, detectives, we have no depositor with that last name."

"Thank you, Mr. Mercier. We appreciate your time."

"Happy New Year," Mercier offered.

"Happy New Year," Tiffin repeated. North was already across the lobby and heading for the car.

"Why your hurry, Brick," Tiffin said as he jumped into the passenger seat.

"Did you see the sign on the door when we entered?"

"There were a bunch of signs at the bank. Which sign are you talking about?"

North crushed out his cigarette in the ashtray and lit another, "The one that said that the bank was closing at noon today for the holiday."

"Doesn't mean everyone is closing at noon."

"That doesn't mean they're not," North retorted.

162

Brick drove down the block where a police callbox stood at the corner. Using his key, he opened the box and picked up the receiver.

"LaSalle Harbor Police."

"Ruth? It's North. Let dispatch know that Tiffin and I are heading to the Inter-City Bank."

"I will do," she said, then added, "be safe."

"Thanks, doll." Hanging up the receiver and closing the callbox, he climbed back into the Ford.

"Where to, Brick?" Tiffin asked as he lit a cigarette.

"I told dispatch that we'd head over to Inter-City Bank. Then, let's plan on visiting People's Savings and wrap up with the LaSalle Harbor State Bank if we need to."

Inter-City Bank was much smaller than the bank they had just left. They approached a desk at the rear of the lobby. Tiffin and North pulled their jackets back to reveal the badges on their belts, "Good morning," Tiffin began, "We're interested in seeing if Doctor Gerald Doolen is doing business with your bank."

"Doolen?" the middle-aged bank manager asked, "the name is not familiar."

North lit a cigarette, "Perhaps you can check the bank's records for us. It is rather important."

"We not only hold our customer's money, but we also take great pride in holding their confidentiality."

Leaning down with his fists on the manager's desk, North looked into the man's eyes, "We're not talking Capone, here. We're talking about a doctor from Iowa who moved here within the past few months."

The manager sat tall in his chair, "I'm sorry, gentlemen, but without a court order, I can't give you any client information."

163

Blowing smoke toward the ceiling, North stood his full six-two and looked down, "This is official police business. Perhaps we should haul your smug ass in for interfering with a murder investigation. Of course, that would make you an accessory. Tiffin, why don't you cuff," he took a moment and glanced at the name plaque, "Mr. Krieger."

"Now, you just wait one minute!" Krieger jumped to his feet, "You can't arrest me!"

Tiffin grabbed Krieger's right arm and snapped a handcuff on his wrist, "Damn shame to get locked up on New Year's Eve. Probably be early next week before you're arraigned."

The handful of customers in the lobby all turned and looked at the commotion. North smiled, "Don't worry folks, your money is probably safe."

"Alright!" Krieger said, "Get this handcuff off of me, and I'll check the records."

Released from the cuff, Krieger walked to a counter behind the teller windows. North and Tiffin followed. Krieger went through the card file two times, "There's no account for anyone with that name."

North tipped the Stratosphere, "Thank you for our cooperation."

"I'll have your badges for this!" Krieger shouted.

"And I'll have the Bank Examiner's here by the end of this week," North smiled.

"There's no way you could pull that off," Krieger said smugly.

North looked down at the manager, "The Michigan Bank Examiner and I served in the war together. He always takes my calls."

Krieger looked nervous, "Okay, fine. Just get out, and we can forget the whole thing."

"We appreciate your cooperation." The detectives stepped out of the bank and into the street.

Tiffin gave North a quizzical look as he stepped into the car, "You know the state's Bank Examiner?"

"Think about it, Tiff. How the hell would I know the Bank Examiner?"

"But you said you served together."

"You think Krieger is going to call him to see if I do?" North laughed as he pushed the shifter into first and pulled away from the curb. They found a parking spot near the corner of State and Pleasant near People's Savings. Tiffin used the callbox across from the savings and loan to notify dispatch of their location. The clock over the door showed a quarter past ten.

"Good morning, gentlemen. May I help you?" The question was posed by an attractive blonde behind the teller window.

North displayed his badge, "We have a question regarding someone who may be a customer. Is there someone we can talk to?"

"Pardon me for a moment." The teller smiled and walked toward a door located behind her, "Excuse me, Mr. Kelm, there are a couple of police officers who have a question." She turned back to her window, "He will be right with you."

A man of some sixty years walked out of the office and past the swinging gate into the lobby, "I'm Thomas Kelm. How may I help you?"

"I'm Detective North; this is my partner, Detective Tiffin. We're interested in speaking with someone who may have an account here."

"Who might that be," Kelm asked agreeably.

"A Gerald Doolen. Moved here from Iowa within the past few months."

"Jerry? Sure. He deposited a rather substantial cashier's check when he moved here. He comes in occasionally to withdraw money for his living expenses."

North pulled his notepad and pencil from his pocket, "You wouldn't happen to have an address for Mr. Doolen, would you?"

"Let me see what we have on file," Mr. Kelm walked behind the counter and pulled a file cabinet drawer open. After flipping through manilla folders, he came back with a slip of paper, "Here you go. I hope this helps." Kelm handed the paper to North, who glanced at it.

"I thank you for your time."

"Happy New Year!" Kelm called after them as they walked out of the building.

"What did we get?" Tiffin asked, the excitement evident in his voice.

"Squat," North said as he balled up the paper and tossed it onto the floorboard of the Ford.

"How so?"

"Doolen gave his address as nine forty-three Morrison Avenue."

"So, what's the problem?"

"If I remember back to my days as a beat cop, Morrison is one block long and begins and ends in the one-thousands."

Tiffin shook his head, "This guy is slicker than snot."

Chapter 17

After a lengthy lunch at the Trophy Room, the detectives spent the rest of the afternoon knocking on doors along and around Morrison Avenue on the off chance that Doolen might have given the correct street name but the wrong house number. No such luck. "I'm telling you," North said as he lit another cigarette, "if he's our killer, he's living near where the bodies were found and not halfway across town."

"I don't know how smart this one is. Doolen was dumb enough to open a savings account in his own name."

"It was the only thing he could do if he had a cashier's check made out to that name."

Tiffin looked out the window toward the sun that was beginning its slow descent into the Lake, "Looks like it's time for me to be heading home. Kaye's going to be looking for my help."

"The life of a hen-pecked man," North smiled.

"You are going to come over, aren't you?" Not surprisingly, Tiffin's comment came out more of a plea than a question.

"I don't know. I'm not much into parties, and I'm certainly not into getting fixed up with someone."

"You have some drinks, we talk, midnight comes, we blow party horns, and we welcome fifty-eight."

North's voice took on a stern quality, "I'll think about it."

"Kaye has invited someone she's certain you'll find interesting."

"I said I'll think about it. Enough said." North turned the Mainline toward the Safety Building. Inside they caught Chief Cummings up on their progress.

"Progress? What progress," Cummings used his thumb to tamp the tobacco down into the bowl of his pipe. "You found where the guy has his savings account. Not much work for a couple of ace detectives. Maybe I should call Uher back up; he couldn't do any worse. Shit, by accident, he might come up with something."

North, being one who never took well to being chastised, nodded and walked to his desk, where he crushed the Strastophere onto his head. "Where are you going, North?" Cummings asked.

"Out." North turned off his desk lamp and walked down the stairs toward the lobby.

Cummings turned to Tiffin, "And what are you going to do?"

With a shrug, Tiffin looked at his boss, "I'm going to go home and help my wife get ready for our party tonight. I'll be back on this after the holiday."

"I should bust both of you back to Patrolman Second Class for insubordination," there was just a hint of a smile on the chief's lips.

"Happy New Year, Pete."

"Happy New Year, Barry. Now, get out of here before I change my mind."

Tiffin walked out the back door just in time to see North's pickup turn onto Main. He tried to think what he was going to tell Kaye.

Like most days, Gatto was waiting at the backdoor when Brick pulled into the drive. "Waiting for your meal ticket, are you bub?" Once inside, he collected the mail that had been deposited through the slot in the front door and read through it while swallowing a shot of bourbon. He then poured himself a second shot to sip as he watched the cat push its dinner plate across the floor.

About seven-thirty, North did a quick perusal of the kitchen. Bad planning had left the cupboard reminiscent of Mother Hubbard's. North grabbed his jacket and pulled it over the .38 slung under his arm. With the Stetson on his head, he climbed into the Dodge and headed into town. Much to his consternation, almost everything was closed for the holiday. There were lights and a couple of cars at Arthur's Drive-In at Niles and Washington. He pulled under the canopy and was studying the menu when a carhop ran up, "We'll be closing soon. Do you know what you want?"

"Honestly, nothing is hitting me," he said in the carhop's direction.

"Do you want to try the Paul Bunyon steak sandwich?" the waitress whose nametag read 'Jesslyn.' offered.

"I think I'll pass," North pulled a half dollar out of his pocket and handed it to the young carhop. "Thank you."

"You're giving me a tip? But you haven't ordered anything!"

"Is that okay?" North said sarcastically.

The young woman smiled, "Of course! Happy New Year, sir."

North pushed the gear shifter into reverse and backed out of the drive-in. He began to aimlessly drive through LaSalle Harbor as he thought about what might have been if Sylvia had lived. North did not live with regrets, and he seldom speculated about the what-might-have-been moments in life. But, he found himself pondering life with Sylvia if she had lived. He was not forming mental images. Instead, he thought about walks on the beach, sharing life, and evenings in bed.

Without having given it much conscious thought, he found himself driving down Hunter Drive. North parked down the street from five twenty-two and didn't pay much if any attention to the red-over-white Plymouth in the drive. The storm door swung outward as he walked up. "Brick!" Kaye Tiffin exclaimed. "I'm so glad you decided to come."

North plastered a strained smile on his face, "I was worried that if I didn't, you might hurt your husband."

"I've been married to Barry long enough," she reached up and kissed North's cheek, "to know how to get rid of a body."

He looked around, "Speaking of bodies, where are all your guests?"

"Everyone just went downstairs. I've got to grab a couple of things; you know your way?"

He nodded, walked through the kitchen and down the basement stairs. Two couples that Brick did not know were seated on the end of the den in what appeared to be a deep conversation. Tiffin was chatting with a tall brunette at the bar on the opposite end of the room. "Here's your Gimlet. Hope I made it right."

"I'm certain it'll be fine."

Tiffin looked at North as he stepped into the room, "Brick, you remember Miss Arquette from the airport, don't you?"

Suzette turned and smiled, "Detective North," she said with her customary breathiness, "it's so good to see you again."

"It's nice to see you, Miss Arquette." He offered her his hand, which she softly squeezed before letting it go.

Tiffin smiled, "I'd told Kaye about the woman that saved you after Lucky Como shot me last summer, and she went out to the airport and invited her to the party."

"Barry?" Kaye's voice came down the stairs, "I could use a hand."

Once Tiffin had left the room, North looked at Suzette, "Do they know that we've seen each other since last July?"

Suzette gave a playful laugh, "No. Kaye came in and told me that she was your friend and thought we might enjoy getting together at this party."

North lit a cigarette, "And you said yes?"

"I wouldn't have if she'd been trying to fix me up with anyone but you."

"Do you want to get fixed up?"

"I did want to see you again, so this seemed like the perfect way to do so." Before he allowed her to pull him toward a love seat near the bar, he poured himself a generous portion of Jack Daniel's. North lit a Pall Mall and absent-mindedly picked a piece of tobacco off his lip, "When did she come to see you?"

"A week or so before Christmas."

"So, before I ever called the airport to make reservations to fly to Iowa?"

Suzette kissed his cheek, "And before we had our date."

"I see you two are hitting it off," Kaye said as she came into the den carrying a tray of snacks which she put on the low coffee table in the center of the room.

"We've run into each other before," Suzette smiled.

Kaye smiled back, happy that her matchmaking skills were strong. Tiffin entered carrying a plate of eggs, tinged in pink with a piece of salmon on top. He offered one to North.

Brick tried to hold back a look of disgust, "Kaye isn't allowing you into the kitchen, is she Tiff?"

Tiffin shook his head, "You need to try this. It's a pickled deviled egg with lox and dill."

"Lox?"

Suzette reached for an egg, "Smoked salmon." She bit into the treat, "Oh, that's so good! Brick, you should try this."

"Pass, thanks." He looked over at the tray on the coffee table, "What else did Kaye make?"

"There are potato and onion knishes and chicken schnitzel bites. She's got brisket and horseradish sandwiches on pumpernickel coming down in a moment."

"I'll wait for that," North said as he took a pull on the Pall Mall.

As Tiffin went to offer the eggs to their other guests, North turned and whispered to Suzette, "Maybe we should sneak out the backdoor."

"We can't do that. It's New Year's Eve. We're expected to stay to greet the new year."

Kaye returned with the promised sandwiches. "Let me introduce everyone!" Kaye said with great enthusiasm. "Everyone, this is Barry's partner, Brick North. And this is Suzette Arquette; she's the manager at Lakeland Airport!" To North and Suzette, she said, "That's Reuben and Rachel Jacobs; they own Jacob's Hat Shop on Washington." The couple gave a friendly wave. "And our other couple is Leonard and Wilma Connors. Leonard is an engineer with Whirlpool."

Suzette smiled at everyone, "How do you all know each other?"

"We ladies are all in the same book club," Wilma Connors offered.

"You manage the airport?" Rachel Jacobs asked.

"I have since August."

"I don't get it," Mr. Jacobs responded. "Shouldn't that be a man's job?"

Suzette sat up straighter, "You don't think that I'm capable?"

"I think you're taking a job from a man," Jacobs offered defensively.

"You run a millinery shop, aren't you taking a job from a woman?" There was no hint of irony or sarcasm in Suzette's voice.

Mrs. Jacobs put a hand on her husband's leg, "I'm sorry, my husband can be old school in his beliefs. But, I think what you're doing is wonderful."

"Let's eat before our goodies get cold," Kaye said to change to subject.

North poured more Jack Daniel's. He was impressed by Suzette's pluck. He grinned; she could hold her own, and he admired that.

The evening continued with the couples breaking into teams. The Tiffin's teamed up with North and Suzette as they played round after round of charades. While not Brick's idea of a good time, he thoroughly enjoyed watching Suzette. She was animated and excited to act out the clues and enthusiastic in calling out answers.

At a quarter past eleven, Tiffin turned on the TV in the corner and worked at tuning it to eliminate as much of the static as possible. After playing with the rabbit ears, he finally got a moderately clear picture on the pink and cream Philco's fourteen-inch screen. "Clairol, on behalf of the hairdressers of America, presents Guy Lombardo and his Royal Canadians from the Grill Room of the Roosevelt Hotel in New York City. Now, Mr. Guy Lombardo…"

While Lombardo ran through popular songs and the screen showed couples dancing on a crowded floor, the ladies chatted, and Tiffin showed the men the cold room turned safe room where Kaye and his children had hidden several months before. "Holy shit," Leonard Connors said as he admired the handiwork, "if you hadn't shown me, I wouldn't have ever found that space."

"I installed it based on an idea from Ian Fleming's James Bond book, 'Casino Royale.' I never thought we'd ever use it for anything other than storage."

As midnight approached, all eyes turned toward the Philco, "We take you now to Time's Square. Seventy-five feet above the New York Times Building is the ball which, as it drops, marks the end of nineteen fifty-seven and the beginning of nineteen fifty-eight. Here it goes!" Along with the crowd in Time's Square, the guests in the Tiffin's basement called out, ten, nine, eight, seven, six, five, four, three, two, one. Happy New Year!"

As the Royal Canadians played Auld Lang Syne, everyone turned and gave their partner a deep kiss. Suzette's soft, warm lips overwhelmed North's senses. His every care and thought evaporated as she flirtatiously sucked on his lower lip.

"We've stayed until midnight," he whispered in her ear. "Why don't you come home with me?"

"I was thinking about having you come up to my apartment."

He smirked, "Only if you have that white teddy you wore last summer."

"I think I can find it."

Chapter 18

New Years morning was as peaceful as any Brick could remember. He and Suzette slept late; her north-facing bedroom window and the sun's low angle allowed him to sleep later than he usually would have.

Suzette brought a cup of coffee into the bedroom and place it on the nightstand. "Good morning, sleepyhead," she kissed him gently on the forehead.

"Good morning, doll." North pushed himself up on an elbow and gave her a kiss as he reached for the coffee. "How long you been up?"

"Long enough to get the coffee going and freshen up."

"Let me splash some water on my face, then I'll collect my clothes from the other room."

"I folded your clothes and put them on the chair in the corner," she used her head to point toward a brocade overstuffed chair in the corner of her bedroom. "Your gun and holster are on the bottom of the pile," she added with a smile.

"I wasn't planning to spend the night; I don't have anything with me."

"You'll find a new toothbrush and comb on the shelf in the bath. I did a little shopping after Christmas and found you a shirt and pants along with some new boxers and a pair of socks. They're in the second drawer down in the dresser."

"How did you know what size to buy?" he sat on the edge of the bed and stretched.

"You're not the only one who can do detective work. I snooped around your house last Saturday morning while you went to the store." Suzette stopped and examined the wounds on his right side, "The newer scar, that's from where Como shot you?"

"That's the one."

"This older scar," she traced it with the tip of her finger, "is that from the war?"

North cast his eyes downward. "I really don't like to talk about the war," he said defensively.

Suzette sat down next to him on the bed, "You were talking about the war last night."

"We didn't talk about the war," North said with a slightly agitated tone to his voice.

"No, we didn't talk about the war, but you did in your sleep. It's okay. It really is okay."

North was startled. He recalled the dream. He just never realized that he was vocal in his sleep. "What did I say?"

"A lot of mumbling about a church and blockading the doors and the Krauts outside. You seemed frightened."

Other than to Tiffin, he had never spoken to anyone about this. The ancient fight or flight mechanism built into every person began to well up within him. Suzette sensed his tension and pulled him close.

North took a deep breath. Suzette's arms felt comforting. "I was frightened. I was sure I was going to die. The soldier I was with did when a grenade came crashing through a window and exploded."

"How did you get out?" Suzette's words were soothing.

"I threw myself behind the ancient oak altar. The shrapnel and blast went around me. The explosion caused a wall at the rear of the church to collapse. I escaped in the confusion of dust and falling timbers."

"Oh, my God! I'd have nightmares too."

North gave an involuntary shudder, "You must think I'm insane for still dwelling on this a dozen years later."

"I think you're the bravest man I know," she kissed him on the cheek. "Can I ask one question? You don't have to answer if you don't want to."

"Okay, sure." Part of him felt like he was going to regret saying yes.

"Who's Adele?"

"Pardon me?"

"Adele, you called out to Adele in your sleep."

North swallowed hard. He was sitting naked next to a beautiful woman, and she was asking him about a woman he was dreaming about. "A German woman I met."

Suzette nodded her understanding, "You met her during the war?"

"No," he said honestly, "sometime after the war had ended."

"I want you to know that you can always tell me what you're feeling. You don't have to hide any part of you from me."

He looked down at himself, "I don't think I'm hiding anything from you." He chuckled.

"I'm serious. I want to know everything about you, and I can only do so if you are open with your thoughts and feelings."

"Sometimes my feeling don't have words attached to them."

"Sometimes couples don't need words," she kissed him softly. "Now, you go clean up while I get breakfast going." She watched him walk into the bathroom, "There are clean towels on the vanity."

"Thanks, doll," he called out as he shut the door.

Showered and dressed, he felt like a new man. The sounds and smells of cooking caught his attention as he carried his coffee cup into the kitchen. "What have you got going here?"

"I'm making a traditional French breakfast for you, or as close as I can. We have *omelette de fromage* made with *Comté Vieux* and *tartine* with butter and strawberry jam. I'm going to have *cafe au lait*, but I imagine you'll just want black coffee."

North lit the critical first cigarette of the day, "You thought of everything." He took a drag on the cigarette, "How did you know that I'd come home with you?"

Suzette cocked her head, "You're joking, right? I knew if you showed up at the Tiffin's, you'd wake up here."

"I admire your optimism," he joked as he picked a piece of tobacco off his lip and rolled it between his fingers.

She laid breakfast on the table, "Have you ever heard it said that trust is the most intimate thing a couple can share?"

North held his fork over the omelet, "I've thought about being intimate enough times. But I haven't thought much about intimacy."

"I'm trying to say that I'm glad you could trust me with your nightmare. Do you have that dream a lot?"

"I've relived that Christmas morning hundreds of times over the years."

"So the answer is yes."

"There are many nightmares I relive. They are all around December of forty-four when I got separated from my unit."

"I go back to what I said in the bedroom; you are the bravest man I know."

North looked across the table, "I don't know about that."

"It's not for you to say," Suzette took a bite of her *tartine*. "You trusted me with your secret; can I share mine?'

"What have you got?"

"I was married once," she said as she pushed the omelet around on the plate with her fork.

"That doesn't bother me, doll."

"Some men want to believe they're the first one and the only one."

North looked into her eyes, "I think it would be more important to know that I'm the last."

"Is it wrong to say that I'm not sure I'm ready to settle down?"

"No, doll, because I'm not ready to settle down."

She smiled, and North was sure he saw a small crack in her confident veneer, "If you were, you know, ready to settle down, would I be in the race?"

"You'd be the only one running.

By noon when North exited the front door of Suzette's apartment house, it was twenty degrees below freezing. The Dodge turned over slowly but finally started about the time he feared the six-volt battery was about out of juice. He drove down the alley and onto Catalpa before turning onto Colfax toward his house. Gatto, who had remained inside when he'd left the night before, bolted out the door and ran toward the bluff as North pushed the backdoor open. "It's cold; you'll be back!" He shouted as the marmalade cat disappeared into the brush.

He poured a couple of fingers of Old Quaker into a coffee cup and sat at the kitchen table thinking about the brunette. Friday night, she had asked him what he found attractive about her. He had quipped about her looks and assertiveness, but there was so much more. There was a connection that he couldn't put his finger on. It just was. By the time he had finished the bourbon, Gatto was screaming at the door to be let back into the house.

Thursday morning found North and Tiffin meeting with the acting District Attorney going over the details of the Kelly George case, "I've got to tell you, detectives," the DA took a deep pull on his cigarette, "we've got a pretty slim case against Mr. George."

"But you can get a conviction, right?" Tiffin asked anxiously.

"Maybe, with a sympathetic jury. Honestly, I wouldn't even bring this to trial if I wasn't getting pressure from the City Council."

North shook his head, "What's the Council got to do with this?"

"You've probably read that they've voted to tear down Tin City, right?"

"I'm not getting the connection," North snapped the lid to his Zippo closed.

"They've used crime and especially Mr. Cudlip's murder to help make the case to shut it down."

"I don't get it," Tiffin interjected, "won't a similar camp be set up somewhere else?"

The DA nodded, "True enough. But between you and me, the city has already made a deal to sell that property to a company that's going to make cardboard boxes."

North took a drag on the Pall Mall, "I wonder how much money changed hands to make that happen."

"I wouldn't know. And considering the corruption that was happening around here, I don't want to know," the DA closed the file that had been lying open on his desk. "This goes to trial in two weeks. It wouldn't hurt if you could come up with something more substantial."

There weren't any more people willing to talk about Kelly George with him behind bars than there were when he was free. The only one who seemed keen to open up was Harry Fuchs, the manager at Tin City, "Shit, I'm eighty years old, just found out I'm losing my job and the place where I live. So anything Machine Gun might do to me will probably be a favor."

Tiffin offered the elderly man a cigarette, which he glommed. "Where are you going to go?"

"I don't got no idea. I've got a daughter somewhere in Massachusetts, but I ain't talked to her in thirty years."

"Damn shame, Fuchs," North's sarcasm was especially pointed. "We're here because you said you had information on Mack Cudlip's murder that you didn't share before. So, you going to whine like an old lady, or are you going to tell us what it is?"

"Machine Gun told me that he killed Mack."

"Just like that?" North asked incredulously. "He just walked up and said, 'Harry, you should know that I killed Cudlip.'"

"Not exactly. I was in the kitchen, and I heard him talking to a couple of the men about offing Mack. So I walked into the dining hall, and point-blank asked him to repeat what he had said."

North scratched a couple of notes, "What did he say?"

"He said that Mack owed him a few bucks, and when he couldn't pay, he offed him."

"What were his exact words?" Tiffin asked.

"He said, 'That fucker thought he could get away with not paying me, so I made him an example to the others who owe me money.'"

"But, did he tell you directly that he killed Cudlip?" North pressed.

"Yup. When I asked what he meant, he got a happy look on his face and said, 'I killed the bastard.'"

Tiffin gave the man a sympathetic look, "We need you to testify at his trial. You up to that?"

"Hell, yeah. When's the slimy bastard going to court?"

"About two weeks from now. A summons server will bring you a subpoena with the exact date and time." North crushed his cigarette out on the snow-covered dirt.

"Good," Fuchs offered. "I can't wait to see him in the hoosegow."

North smiled as he turned toward the car, "The men up in Jackson," referring to the state penitentiary, "like to bring guys like Kelly down to size."

Back in the squad room, they caught the chief up on what had transpired. "Out of the blue, this Fuchs just called? That's a spot of good luck."

"The DA was happy to hear about it," Tiffin said as he poured a cup of coffee.

Cummings chuckled, "I bet he was. The case was hearsay. So, what are you ace detectives up to now?"

North looked up at the clock; it was half-past eleven, "It's been a full morning. I think I might go to lunch."

"You two still swilling whiskey at the Trophy Room?" the chief asked in a non-accusatory fashion.

Tiffin used his head to point at North, "He swills the whiskey. I normally get a burger."

"Grab you hats, boy. I think I'm going to join you today, and I just might buy. Let me get my coat," Cummings turned toward his office. When he stepped back into the squad room, he looked toward North, "Why are you just standing there? Call dispatch and tell them that we're going to lunch."

Chapter 19

Friday, January third, arrived bitterly cold. The warm moist air escaping from North's nose and mouth froze the moment he exhaled. Ice formed around his nostrils and clung to the stubble on his upper lip. The thermometer outside the kitchen window claimed the air temperature to be seven degrees, but the thirty-mile-per-hour winds off the Lake made it feel like it was twenty below.

He got the pickup started and smoked a cigarette while he waited for the engine to warm. In temperatures this cold, there was not enough moisture in the air to conduct sound. As a freight train lumbered past his backyard, he noticed it was the vibration created by the hundred twenty-five-ton EMD F7 engine that alerted him as it passed and not the sound of the mammoth diesel engine itself.

North sat down on his regular stool at the counter of the Fifth Wheel. He had just taken the first slug of coffee when a man in a grey overcoat took the seat next to him. "There might be a better place to park your ass than at my elbow," North sneered.

"Detective North?" the man asked.

Brick turned and took a serious look at a kid who was probably just old enough to order a beer, "What's it to you?"

"I'm Donald Anderson; I write for the LaSalle Palladium."

"Good for you, kid. Now, if you don't mind, I'm going to eat my breakfast, read the rag you write for, and pretend like you don't exist." North turned back to his mug of coffee.

"I want to verify a couple of facts before my story breaks in the afternoon edition." The reporter pulled a notebook from his pocket and flipped it open. North ignored him. "Can you verify that you are looking for a retired doctor from Iowa as a suspect in the Sand Rabbit murders?"

North slammed the mug down hard enough that coffee leaped from it, "What did you say?"

"I asked if you would confirm that you're searching for a doctor from Iowa in connection to the Sand Rabbit murders."

Working to keep his cool, North lowered his voice, "I don't know what you're talking about, kid, and neither do you."

"I got my information from someone inside your department that says otherwise."

North leaned forward and held his thumb and index finger an inch apart in front of Anderson's nose, "We're this close to wrapping this case up. You tell the world we're looking for some doctor from Iowa, and the man we're after will go so deep we may never find him."

Anderson held a pencil to the notebook, "So it's true."

North reached over and pulled the notepad from the reporter's grasp. "Hey, you can't do that! Freedom of the press is sacrosanct!" Anderson reached for the book. North held him back as he read through the notes.

"You can't print this. But I'll make you a deal. When we catch the killer, I'll give you the exclusive."

"My editor expects thirty column inches on this story by noon today."

"Tell your editor that he can go pound sand up his ass."

The reporter grabbed for the notebook. As he reached, his shoulder came in contact with North's jaw. "That, my friend, is assault on a peace officer. Stand up and put your hands behind your back."

"I brushed your chin with my shoulder."

"Stand up and turn around, or I'll add resisting arrest to the charges." North grabbed Anderson by the shoulder and roughly turned him around. Handcuffs clicked around the reporter's wrists. Grabbing his hat, North directed Anderson through the door and across the street to the Safety Building.

"What have you got, detective?" the duty sergeant asked as he looked down from his desk.

"This is Donny Anderson. I'm charging him with assault on a peace officer. Have someone take him down to the holding cells."

Anderson protested, "I'm a reporter. I know my rights!"

"Good for you, kid. Good for you." North lit a cigarette and walked to the stairs that led up to the squad room. He was waiting in the chief's office when Cummings came in.

"There's probably a good reason you're sitting at my desk," Cummings said as he hung his overcoat and hat on the oak coat stand.

North handed him Anderson's notebook, "You might want to look at this."

A flush rose on Cummings face, "Where the hell did you get this?"

"A reporter from the Palladium by the name of Anderson. He says he got the information from someone here in the department."

"Bloody hell!" Cummings fumed. "Find out who's been feeding him information. I don't care if you have to talk with every officer, janitor, and visitor who's been here in the past couple of weeks." The chief turned his attention back to the notebook, "How did you get this?"

"Mr. Anderson pushed his shoulder into my jaw, so I arrested him for assault."

"He struck you with his shoulder?"

"No, he brushed me with his shoulder, but I wanted to get this," North used his head to point to the notebook, "and get him out of circulation for a while."

Cummings picked up the phone. An operator at the switchboard answered immediately, "How may I help you, chief?"

"Get me Stanley Banyon at the Palladium."

"I'll call you when we have him," she disconnected, and Cummings replaced the handset on the cradle.

North lit a cigarette, "Who's this Banyon?"

The chief reached for a cigarette; North handed him the pack, "Stanley Banyon is the publisher of the Palladium." The phone rang. "Cummings."

"Please hold for Mr. Banyon," there was a click on the line as the call was patched through.

"Pete! What can I do for you?"

"I've got a problem that you can help me with."

"What's that?" Banyon asked as he lit a cigarette.

"Well, Stan, the first thing is I've got one of your reporters in a holding cell."

"What?! Who have you arrested?"

Cummings put his hand over the mouthpiece, "Who did you arrest?" he asked North.

"A kid by the name of Donny Anderson."

"Looks like we've got a cub-reporter by the name of Donny Anderson locked up for assault on a peace officer."

"Anderson? He's not one-forty wet. I don't think he's the type to go around hitting cops."

"He pushed his shoulder into one of my detective's jaws during an argument. You can send someone over to claim him. But let's talk about what led to the altercation."

"I think I have an idea of what's going on, but why don't you tell me," Banyon's tone became very formal.

"If you proceed with the story Anderson is writing; your paper will destroy our chance of solving the murders of three young girls."

"We have a duty to keep the public informed…," Banyon began.

Cumming cut him off, "You have a duty to sell newspapers to raise money for your stockholders. I have an obligation to keep our city safe. My obligation trumps your duty. Once we get our murderer behind bars, we'll give you access to our case files. Hell, the wire services will probably pick up the story you guys write."

There was a pause on the line before Banyon finally answered, "How long have we known each other, Pete?"

"Since I was a rookie cop and you were the cub reporter."

"I've always trusted you to tell me the truth. I'll take your word that we can access your case files when this guy is behind bars."

"And I'll take your word that you won't publish anything until then." Cummings took a deep pull on the Pall Mall and blew smoke toward the ceiling.

"It's a deal," the newspaper publisher answered.

"Let me ask you one more question, Stan."

"What's that?"

"Who fed Anderson the information?"

"I honestly don't know, Pete."

"Will you tell me when you find out?"

There was a pause, "We'll have to wait and see." Banyon ended the call.

Cummings replaced the handset on the cradle, "He's not going to tell us who gave them the information. So you and Tiffin figure out who our gossip is."

"Yes, sir," North walked into the squad room.

Tiffin looked up from his desk, "You were in there a long time. Everything okay?"

"Just ducky." North dropped into his chair, "Someone here let a reporter in on the fact that we're looking for a doctor from Iowa. They were going to run the story this afternoon."

"You're joking, right? That's a leak we can't patch. Doolen will be long gone."

The chief knows the big cheese at the Palladium. They'll sit on the story until we find Doolen. In the meantime, we're not only looking for him; we're looking for our leak."

"Where do we start?" Tiffin looked concerned.

"The chief says we're to interview every officer, janitor, and visitor who's been through here in the last two weeks." North walked over to the urn and was pleasantly surprised to find coffee.

"That could be a lot of people."

"I've weeded it down to just one," North swallowed a mouthful of coffee.

"Uher," Tiffin said under his breath.

"Winner, winner, chicken dinner."

"Have you seen him?"

North picked up the phone. Ruth immediately answered it, "How may I help you, detective?"

"Where's Detective Uher?"

"Let me check. Please hold a moment." Then, after a very brief pause, "Detective Uher checked in at five o'clock this morning and said he would be in the dayroom if needed. He has not checked in again."

"Thank you, Ruth." North turned to Tiffin, "The bastard is in the dayroom." The two made their way to the small room where detectives could catch a nap and where Dan Uher had been living for the past couple of weeks.

North threw the door open as Tiffing hit the light switch. "Rise and shine, Danny boy," North shouted.

"What the hell!" Uher protested, "I was out most the night on a call."

North slammed the door and sat on a cot opposite of Uher, "You've been feeding information to someone at the Palladium."

"Says who?"

"Says the notebook that a reporter loaned me."

"My name's not in that book," Uher retorted.

North leaned forward, "What book is that, Dan?"

190

Uher squirmed a little, "Uh, the book that you're talking about."

"How exactly did Donald Anderson come to talk to you?" Tiffin asked pointedly.

Looking between his two fellow detectives, Uher finally sighed, "He was at a robbery scene I was at, and we got to talking."

"How much did he pay you?" North asked as Uher was answering Tiffin's question.

"What?"

"How much? He's at a robbery scene, and you just start feeding him information about the bodies of three girls found at Cooper-Wells? It sounds to me like you were offered a few bucks in exchange for juicy info."

"Maybe one of the uniforms told him."

"And then we start looking for a doctor from Iowa, and that information hasn't left the detective squad. Where would Anderson have learned of that, Tiff?"

Tiffin exaggeratedly rubbed his chin, "Hmmm. Maybe Uher here needed a few more bucks."

"How much!" North shouted. "How much did you get paid selling information to the reporter?"

"Ten bucks!" Uher shouted back. "Five dollars for each time I shared some information."

North stood and looked down upon Uher, "Those girls' lives were worth a hell of a lot more than ten bucks!"

"Oh, like you've never needed a few dollars," Uher offered defensively.

Tiffin shook his head, "There've been plenty of times I've needed money. I just never thought about betraying my badge to get it."

Uher looked down, "So, what are you going to do now?"

"We're not going to do anything," North said as he looked at Tiffin, who was shaking his head.

"You're not?" Uher sounded relieved.

"No, but you're going to go to the chief and tell him what you've done," North lit a cigarette.

"And if I don't?"

"Then Tiffin and I are going to tell him."

"He's going to fire me!" Uher pleaded.

"No, you fired yourself when you sold information to a reporter. Cummings is just going to make it official," Tiffin offered.

"I'll tell him at the end of the day."

North gave Uher a look of disgust, "You've got five minutes to get in there, or I'll drag your ass in there."

Twenty minutes later, two uniformed officers were leading Uher out of the building. Chief Cummings poked his head out of his office, "Tiffin, North, get your asses in here."

North picked a piece of tobacco off his lip, "What's up, chief?"

"When did you know it was Uher?"

"As soon as I learned the reporter had information that was only known in the squad room."

"You didn't consider any of the other detectives?" Cummings tamped moist tobacco into the bowl of his pipe.

Tiffin shrugged, "There's only six of us in the squad. And only one is going through a divorce and sleeping on a cot here."

"Good work. Now, go find Doolen and let's get this case wrapped up."

"On it, chief!" North said as he and Tiffin walked back to their desks. "You know what this means, don't you, Tiff?"

"That we're a man down on the squad?"

"Well, there's that. I was thinking that with Uher out of the picture, we'll have to start rotating through the nights again."

"And here I thought that Uher was good for nothing."

Chapter 20

In his dream, it was December twenty-second, nineteen forty-four. The sun had just set, and North's company was encamped near Freyneux, France. The battle for the Ardennes was going poorly; the Germans had sent in everything they had in a last-ditch effort to sway the war's outcome. "Mail call," a young PFC whispered as he moved among the troops. "North, Brian," he called out.

"Here!" North responded.

The PFC handed him an envelope that had obviously passed through many hands to get to him. North recognized his father's handwriting on the envelope. He tore it open and pulled out the onion-skin paper that had been enclosed.

"Dear Son, I read daily of the battles that you and your brave companions are fighting in Europe. I don't know where you are, but I hope this letter gets to you and finds you well. I write to tell you that your mother passed away yesterday, November fifteenth, after a brief illness. Her last thoughts were of you and for your safety. Your Aunt Charlotte had been staying with us to help me care for your mother. She will be returning to Ohio after the funeral. I'm sorry to have to share this news in this fashion. I look forward to the war's end and your return. Dad."

North read the note through three more times. "Five weeks! She's been gone five weeks!" He pushed the letter into the breast pocket of his field jacket, stood, and began to walk the perimeter of the encampment. Four members of his rifle company were gathered around a small Sterno fire trying to make hot chocolate out of an emergency ration bar and powdered milk. "Hey, Sarge," one called out, but North couldn't hear him; he was too busy thinking about the last words that he'd had with his mother and the many things he wished he could tell her. Finally, he sat under a hedgerow and, for the first time in many years, cried.

He didn't know when he had fallen asleep; the cold and the absolute silence woke him. His company was gone. He was alone and without his rifle.

"Shit!" he sat up in bed, sweat having saturated the pillow and sheets. He swung his legs off the side of the bed and sat there trying to get his bearings. North reached for the bottle of Old Quaker and swallowed a mouthful. The bourbon burned its way to his stomach. He tried to focus on the Bulova. After staring at the luminous dial for a minute, he decided that either read a quarter of or a quarter past three. Either way, it didn't matter.

Having pulled on some clothes, he and Gatto walked out the side door of the house. The sky was so clear, the stars didn't twinkle. Instead, they, along with the waxing gibbous moon, shone bright and unwavering. He walked along the beach. The ice on the Lake was heavier than it had been in some years. He had been told the ice was almost four feet thick in some places. No ships moved on Lake Michigan. There was no one between him and Chicago, sixty miles across the lake. He felt as alone as he did that night in the Ardennes.

He had walked miles by the time he returned to the house. The cat was curled up at the door, "Come on, you little beggar, get inside and get yourself warmed up." North removed the Mac and his boots before falling onto the bed.

The sun woke him. He looked at the watch on his arm, seven-twenty. North laid there a minute and tried to remember what day it was. "Saturday," he thought to himself as he sank back into the bed. He drifted for just a moment before he sat upright, "Saturday! I've got to get my ass over to Damaske's!"

He quickly washed up and pulled some clothes on. He was rapping at the door of the market by seven forty-five. The butcher opened the door for him, "Good morning, detective. I've got to tell you, I really wasn't sure you were going to come this morning."

"I wouldn't miss this. I'm more than just a little curious about your sausage casing customer."

"You think he's up to no good, do you?" Damaske asked.

"I don't know what he's up to. But, he's willing to pay a premium price for hundreds of feet of something few would buy. It's just hinky enough to be worth looking into."

The butcher fixed North up with a clean white apron, a pair of garters to hold his sleeves up and away from his wrists, and a white paper garrison cap emblazoned with the words, "Damaske's Market" on the side. The apron covered the .38 that North wore in the front of his pants. "The guy comes in right about eight, so about the time we unlock the door, he should be walking in."

"Where's the box of casings?"

Damaske walked North to the cooler and pulled the door open. He pointed to an eight-inch square box on a shelf to the left.

"Three hundred feet of sausage casing fits in that tiny box?"

"It's incredibly thin."

The chime over the door tinkled as the first customers walked in. As agreed, Damaske walked into the back room and out of sight of the

196

meat case. An older woman walked up to the counter, "Where's Mr. Damaske," she asked.

"He's taking the day off," North replied. "What can I help you with?"

"I'm looking for a nice fryer. Maybe three pounds or so."

North looked around the case, obviously unaware of what the woman was asking for. "A chicken!" she exclaimed. "You're not a butcher, are you?"

"No, ma'am," North answered honestly. "I'm just helping out this morning."

"Well, they'd do better if they brought in someone who knew a chicken from a hole in the ground!" She pointed at a bird in the case, "Just give me that one."

North took the chicken, wrapped it in white butcher paper, placed a piece of tape on the poorly wrapped package, and wrote 50¢ with a waxed pen on the paper before handing it to her.

"You didn't even weigh that!"

"It's okay. You're getting a good deal." He said as he tried to get her away from the counter. She took the chicken and walked away, grumbling as she went.

A well-groomed man of about sixty years approached the counter. "Where's the regular guy?"

"He's taking the day off," North replied. "What can I do for you?"

"He keeps a box of sausage casings for me."

"Sausage casings, you say? Let me see." North walked around the front of the meat case pretending to look as he moved close to the man.

North was just two feet away when the Wolfe boys ran toward him, "Detective North!" Jack yelled. "Do you work here, too?"

The older man's eyes widened as he turned and ran toward the front door. North was just behind him. The man would have made it outside if he hadn't tripped over the woman with the chicken. Instead, North reached out and grabbed the collar of the man's blue wool jacket.

"You and I need to talk," North said as he hauled him toward the backroom.

"Who are you?!"

North reached into his pocket and produced his badge, "As the kid said a moment ago, I'm Detective North of the LaSalle Harbor Police Department."

"You can't arrest me! There's nothing illegal about buying sausage casing."

As they entered the stockroom of the market, North asked Damaske, "Do me a favor and call the police department. Tell them that I need a couple of uniformed officers."

The butcher nodded and walked toward the front of the store. North used his head to point toward a crate, "Sit."

The man repeated, "You can't arrest me for buying sausage casings."

"I'm not arresting you. At the moment, I'm holding you for questioning. Now, sit."

"Questions about what?" the man said defensively.

"Well, first, why don't you tell me your name," North said as he pulled the apron and sleeve garters off.

"I'm not doing anything wrong. I don't have to tell you my name or anything for that matter."

"Look, friend, I'm not looking to jack you up," North lit a smoke.

"Am I free to go?" the man's face was beet red.

"Not until you answer a couple of straightforward questions for me," North absent-mindedly picked a piece of tobacco off his lip, rolled it between his fingers, and flicked it onto the wooden floor.

"Fine," the man paused for a moment, "Emerson. The name's Ralph Emerson."

North's tone dripped sarcasm as he replied, "Okay, Mr. Emerson, that wasn't so hard, was it? Now, tell me about the sausage casings."

"What's to tell? I like sausage."

"Sure, I do too, when it's sausage. You're buying just the casing. What're you doing with it?"

"None of your damn business. Now, I'm leaving," Emerson began to rise.

North pushed him back down, "As a matter of courtesy, I haven't cuffed you. I can remedy that. Now sit down and answer my questions."

"I fry it up and feed it to my dog. Satisfied?"

North mulled the response for a moment, "Honestly, no. You could buy fifty pounds of pork for what you're willing to give for the casings. What the hell are you doing with the stuff, Mr. Emerson?"

"You wouldn't understand. Now, unless I'm under arrest, I'm leaving."

There was nothing North could hold Emerson on. The man could spend his money any way he wanted.

"Get the hell out of here," North said through clenched teeth.

"I need the box of sausage casings I came for," Emerson replied.

"Damaske," North shouted.

The butcher stuck his head into the stock room, "Detective?"

"What do you pay for that box of casings?"

"A hank of casings costs me about seventy cents."

North turned to Emerson, "And you're willing to give twenty bucks for it. It doesn't make sense."

"I meant it when I said you wouldn't understand," Emerson said in a condescending tone.

"You might be right. But I understand enough to know that you're not being honest with me."

"May I have my casings and go now?"

North nodded toward Damaske, "Give him the casings."

Damaske returned from the cooler with the box, "That'll be twenty dollars."

Emerson pulled out his wallet and handed the butcher two ten-dollar bills.

"You aren't the only butcher in town, Damaske. I'm taking my business elsewhere."

The butcher shrugged, "Your choice."

North grabbed his jacket and the Stetson and followed Emerson out the door. "You don't need to follow me, detective. I'm leaving."

"That's okay, Emerson; I'll walk you out."

With the box of casings under his arm, Emerson moved to a dark blue Buick and climbed in. North walked toward the approaching patrol car. As the Buick drove by, he noticed the black and white Iowa plate on the bumper. "Stop him!" he shouted to Brodeur as the Buick sped away.

North climbed into his pickup as the patrol car, siren screaming, began pursuit. By the time North caught up with them, Emerson's car had slid off the slick lakefront roadway and was stuck in a small ditch. He tried frantically to rock the vehicle free by swiftly shifting between reverse and first. The officers approached the Buick with guns at the ready. "Out of the car," Brodeur shouted authoritatively.

As Emerson climbed out of the car, North approached. "Doctor Doolen, I presume."

Chapter 21

Two hours later, Tiffin and North had Doolen in the interrogation room. North examined the Iowa driver's license from Doolen's wallet, "Do you prefer Gerald Doolen, or should we stick with Ralph Waldo Emerson?"

"I'd prefer to know why I have been arrested," a highly agitated Doolen answered. "My wife is very ill, and I need to get home to her."

"According to your driver's license, you're from Davenport, Iowa."

"Lot's of people are from Davenport."

North lit a cigarette, "You had privileges at Mercy Hospital until you retired, correct?"

"There are dozens of doctors who do." What's your point?

"If I mention cabinet fourteen in the hospital archives, would you know what I'm referring to?" North took a deep drag on the cigarette that was seemingly glued to the corner of his lip.

"How the hell should I know what that is?" Doolen said defensively.

"Seems like you should, Doctor. You signed the register book to access that cabinet dozens and dozens of times between fifty-two and fifty-five."

"Anyone could have signed my name to that register."

"What are the odds that a photograph of the signature in the register would match the signature on your driver's license?" Tiffin asked as North crushed out his cigarette and lit another.

"I wouldn't know." Doolen looked between the detectives, "Gentlemen, I really must go. My wife is very ill, and she doesn't know where I am."

"Why were you looking through the blood type archives, doctor?" North demanded in a voice that shook the glass window in the door.

"Fine. I was doing research."

"Research, doctor? You weren't looking for a particular blood type to help a patient?"

Doolen cockily sat forward, "Just research. Now, I'm going to go care for my wife." He began to stand.

"Sit your ass down!" North commanded. "We haven't even begun our interview." He opened his worn leather notepad and flipped through the pages. Finally, North found what he was looking for and studied the page for a moment. "Tell me about Linda Kniebes."

"Who? How should I know?"

"Linda was a fifteen-year-old Girl Scout who took part in a blood typing program at Mercy Hospital. She had type O-negative blood. Disappeared from her home in Davenport on June twelfth, fifty-two. Her remains are in our morgue."

A bead of sweat appeared on the doctor's forehead.

"How about Patricia Eber, sixteen. She was in the same Girl Scout troop as Miss Kniebes. Had O-negative blood. Disappeared from Davenport late May of fifty-three?" North paused. "Don't remember Patricia? We have her remains; maybe that would jar your memory."

"Why are you doing this?" Doolen bellowed. "I don't know what you're going on about."

"No? Hey Tiff, do you find it odd that the good doctor doesn't recall these girls he kidnapped and murdered?"

"Murder?" Doolen pleaded, "You haven't got anything on me."

"Whoa," Tiffin exclaimed as he looked at his partner, "That's not the same as I didn't do it."

North smiled, "No, Tiff, it isn't." He turned back to Doolen, "Do you remember Susan Crouse? Girl Scout from Eldridge, Iowa? She and her troop did the blood typing program at Mercy Hospital. Had type O-negative blood. Went missing June eighteenth of fifty-four. Remember Susan?"

"I don't remember her or the other girls!"

"You believe him, Tiff?" North asked as he picked a piece of tobacco off his lip.

"Not a word, Brick. I think he's been lying since we walked in."

"What say we let him sweat in a holding cell for a while. Then, you and I can go catch lunch." North stood and walked toward the door.

"NO!" Doolen roared. "My wife is home, alone, and sick. I must get home to her."

"We'll send a medic to your home to look after her. But you aren't going anywhere but a cell until you talk." North pulled open his notepad, "Now tell me, where's your wife."

Broken, Doolen leaned forward and put his head on his forearms, "Ten-nineteen Pine at the corner of Third."

"What's your wife's name?" Tiffin asked compassionately.

"Doris."

"Doris? What was her maiden name?" North's pencil hovered above the pad.

"Schaus."

North looked down at the doctor, "The house is in her maiden name, is it?"

"It belongs to her father's brother. He's living with his son in Florida. We're in the process of buying it from him."

North dropped back into the chair, "You're getting talkative, Jerry. Mind if I call you Jerry?"

"You go take care of my wife, and maybe, just maybe, I'll talk more. Right now, I'm done talking."

Tiffin and North left Doolen sitting in the interrogation room. Two officers walked in and led the doctor to the elevator and the holding cells in the basement. North picked up the phone. "How may I help you, detective?"

"I need to speak with Doctor Howard. Find him and ring me when you've got him." North hung up before the operator could answer him.

One cup of coffee and two cigarettes later, the phone rang, "North."

"Hold for Doctor Howard," there were a couple of clicks on the line as they were connected.

"Mel?" North asked, "Sorry to bother you on a Saturday."

"What have you got?"

"We're holding a man for questioning. He insists his wife is extremely ill and alone. I told him that we'd send someone to check on her."

"And you thought of me!" Howard was nearly as fluent in sarcasm as North, "Where am I going?"

"Ten-nineteen Pine, the corner of Third."

"I'll let you know what I find."

"We might be at the Trophy Room if we're not at the Safety Building."

"Have a scotch and soda for me."

North wrinkled his nose, "Not on your life!"

Howard laughed, "I'm on my way."

North stood and walked to the coatrack, where he grabbed the Stratosphere and crushed it on his head.

"That hat starting to feel like it's yours yet?" Tiffin joked as he slipped on his overcoat.

"I wore that Bradmore for almost ten years. It'll be a while before this one is properly broken in."

"How long do you figure that'll take?"

North smiled, "Maybe ten years."

Tiffin had just bitten into his hamburger when the phone at Trophy Room rang. Charlie picked it up and called to the detectives, "Got Doc Howard on the phone for one of you guys."

North tossed back his second shot and walked to the phone, "What have you got Doc?"

"You need to get here right now!" The doctor sounded shook.

"What's up?"

"Just get here." The line went dead.

North pulled his suit jacket over the holster that hung under his arm, "Eat up, Tiff. The doc needs us right away."

Ten-nineteen Pine Street was a neat two-story frame house on a corner lot. North recognized Howard's Buick Roadmaster in the drive. Behind the Roadmaster was the ambulance from the local mortuary. The detectives stepped through the open front door.

Except for the floral wallpaper and lace curtains, the parlor looked like a hospital room. Lying on a hospital bed was a frail-looking woman who appeared to be only semi-conscious. Rubber tubes ran from her chest to a homemade machine that buzzed loudly. Blood ran out of her body, into the machine, and back to her body.

"What the hell is that?" North asked Doc Howard as he entered the room.

"Looks like someone has made her a dialyzer machine."

"A who?" Tiffin asked as he looked at the contraption.

"An artificial kidney," Howard lifted the metal lid of the device. Inside, blood ran through what looked like sausage casing wrapped around a revolving drum and submerged in a liquid. The blood exiting the dialyzer entered a centrifuge which was powered by a washing machine motor before it was sent back into Mrs. Doolen.

"Holy shit, doc. This looks like Dr. Frankenstein works here." Tiffin exclaimed.

Doc Howard looked at the dialyzer and shook his head, "This is absolute genius! Whoever built this is not only mechanically inclined but understand nephrology."

"Neph who?" North looked up from his notepad.

"The study of kidneys," Howard said over his shoulder as he looked at the machine.

Tiffin shook his head, "So this is a unique invention?"

207

"No, whoever did this built on the designs of Dr. Willen Kolff, who invented the revolving drum dialyzer back in the forties. But, this design solves a problem with the Kolff design."

"What problem?" North asked, actually surprised in his interest in the contraption.

"The dialyzer removes toxins by running the blood through an electrolytic solution, but it can't remove the excess fluids. This centrifuge device removes the excess fluid," Howard pointed to a glass jar under the machine that was collecting a yellow-tinged liquid.

"So the machine is peeing for her, is that it?" North asked.

"Couldn't say it better myself."

"How often would Mrs. Doolen need to be treated on the dialyzer?" Tiffin asked.

"Probably every two to three days."

North looked into the open machine, "So, her blood travels through a hundred feet of sausage casing that's sitting in water, goes through a spin-cycle, and back into her?"

It can't just be water. It's got to have sodium, potassium, calcium, magnesium, chloride," Howard paused as he thought, "and a fair amount of bicarbonate of soda in it."

"So, every time she needs to use this, all the sausage casings and minerals need to be replaced?"

"And this machine has to be meticulously cleaned. This is a huge job. Someone must love this woman dearly." Howard mused.

Tiffin looked up, "You said this solves the problem of excess fluids?"

Howard lit a cigarette, "Yes, that's right."

"What do they do if they don't have this centrifuge thingy?"

"The patient has some of their blood drained."

North nodded his head in understanding, "And if you take blood out, you've got to have something to put back."

"Yes," Howard concurred, "If you give a pint of blood, your body will replace it within a week. No big deal. But a patient on an artificial kidney can't have blood removed every couple of days. Their body couldn't replace it fast enough. That's why the dialyzer is a short-term solution. You place a patient on it in the hopes that whatever kidney disease they have will be cured before the patient dies."

North took a deep pull on the Pall Mall he was smoking, "So, is it possible this woman has been on this machine for three years?"

Howard nodded, "It might be a medical miracle, but it's possible. How can you speculate on the number of years?"

"Because I believe that this woman's husband kidnapped and brought healthy teenaged girls here to have their O-negative transfused into her."

"Our victims from the Copper-Wells building!" Howard exclaimed. "As he was perfecting his machine, he needed to have a reliable supply of blood!"

"How much blood would he have needed to drain from his wife to keep her alive?"

"If he severely limited her fluid intake, and I'm speculating here, but a pint minimally each time."

North nodded his understanding, "Every two or three days, he would have had to take that much from one of the teenagers?"

"Goulish, isn't it?" Howard asked.

Tiffin gave the doctor a confused look, "Why would the girls cooperate?"

"I can only guess he kept them drugged enough to keep them agreeable."

North looked at Doc Howard, "If the girls had drugs in their bloodstream, wouldn't Mrs. Doolen also have ended up drugged?"

"It would be inevitable," Howard agreed.

"Do you think she's drugged now?" Tiffin asked.

"I would say that her current state is probably related more to her general health than chemicals in her system. From the look of things, I'd say that she is in the end stages of life."

"Is there nothing that can be done for her?" Tiffin's voice was full of compassion.

"There has been some solid work done on kidney transplants, but she's too weak for it to be a viable option, even if we had a kidney to give her."

Doc Howard carefully removed the tubes from Mrs. Doolen and, with the ambulance attendants, moved her to a gurney and the dialyzer to the waiting car, "I'll admit her to the hospital. We're going to have a lot of doctors looking at this centrifugal dialyzer."

North picked up the Stetson, which he'd put on a chair, and crushed it onto his head, "Let's go talk to our doctor."

Chapter 22

At the Safety Building, they caught Chief Cummings, who had been in South Bend, up on Doolen and his wife. "So, he created a machine to keep his wife alive?" Cummings mused. "And he kidnapped teenaged girls for their blood. Sounds like something from a horror movie."

North blew a smoke ring toward the ceiling, "Doc Howard says that Mrs. Doolen doesn't have long to live. He says that her system is shutting down, even with the machine."

Cummings packed the bowl of his pipe and sucked the flame from a match into the moist tobacco, "Does Doolen know that?"

"He's a doctor. So I'm guessing he knows the symptoms."

"What has he confessed to?" Cummings blew fragrant smoke into his office.

Tiffin looked at his boss, "Nothing yet."

"Well, you can't hold him for buying sausage casings or building a kidney machine! Get a confession."

"Yes, sir," the detectives said in unison. Back in the squad room, Tiffin whispered, "How, exactly, are we supposed to get a confession from an unwilling man?"

"What's the only thing he seems to care about in this world?"

Tiffin thought for a moment, "His wife."

"Then we get him to confess for his wife's sake." North walked toward the stairs, "You coming?"

"Right behind you."

A young officer sat at the desk outside the corridor that led to the holding cells. North nodded in his direction, "Get Gerald Doolen out and bring him to the interrogation room.

"Yes, detective." While the officer fetched Doolen, the detectives stepped into the small basement-level room used for interrogation. The fluorescent light fixture had just flickered to life when the doctor was brought into the room.

North pointed to the chair opposite his at the table, "Sit down, doctor."

"How's my wife?!" there was panic in his voice.

"She's alive if that's what you mean." North shook a Pall Mall from its red package and offered one to Doolen, who waved it off.

"You don't understand; without me, she'll die."

"Our doctor says that she's near death now. He told me that her systems are shutting down." Tiffin said from his position, standing behind Doolen.

"You don't think I know that?! I'm a doctor for chrissake," he yelled.

"Everybody dies, doc," North said flatly.

"Maybe you've never loved someone like I love Doris. If you did, you'd do everything you could to keep them alive."

North felt the anger rise within him as he thought of Sylvia, "I have loved someone dearly, but I would have never killed for her."

"I didn't kill anybody!"

"Linda Kniebs, Patty Eber, Susan Crouse. Three girls that we know of. How many more have you killed to keep your wife alive?" North leaned forward until his face was within inches of Doolen's.

Doolen yelled back, "How many times do I have to tell you? I didn't kill anybody."

Tiffin held up a finger toward North, who sat back in his chair and took a drag on his cigarette. "The girls died of natural causes, didn't they, doctor?" Tiffin asked.

Doolen turned to face the voice, "Yes! That's right. They died of natural causes."

North jumped in, "And after they died, you buried them the best you could at the abandoned factory."

"That's right. I even said a prayer over each when I buried them."

"Bullshit!" North yelled. "You didn't bury anyone. Instead, you hid their bodies behind boilers and equipment. You dumped them, hoping that by the time they were found, we wouldn't be able to connect them to you."

"Okay, fine! I didn't bury them. Do you feel better being correct?"

"I'll feel better knowing that you'll be locked up for the rest of your natural life if that's what you mean."

"But the girls died of natural causes!"

"Why did you tell us that you didn't know their names?"

"I never called them by name! They were necessary to keep Doris alive. That's all."

"So, what?" Tiffin bristled as he thought about his own daughter, "You called them girl?"

"I didn't call them anything. They were just poor girls who had no future."

North stood and looked down at Doolen, "Those girls would each be young women now. They would probably each be married with some kids of their own. That's a future."

"The world wouldn't miss a handful of poor girls from the wrong side of the tracks," Doolen said smugly. "My wife was an important member of society."

"I know better than most that the justice system typically treats you better if you're rich and guilty than if you're poor and innocent. But not this time, doc." North sat back down, "This time, the jury is going to learn about three girls whose futures were destroyed because you selfishly wanted to keep your wife alive!"

"I didn't kill anybody! Don't you understand? As the other detective said, they died of natural causes."

"I understand that people die when they don't have blood in them. That's natural. What's not natural is how that blood came to be removed. You caused their deaths, doctor. What's the Hippocratic Oath say, 'first, do no harm,' isn't that right? But you did. You did do harm. Those might have been three poor girls with uncertain futures to you. But, they were beloved daughters and sisters to someone else. Who the hell died and made you God, doctor?!"

"I needed to save my wife!" Doolen screamed.

"You kidnapped three young women. You drugged them and systematically drained their life from them. And, your wife is going to die anyway. What did you accomplish? What?!"

"I've made advances in medicine that will keep others alive. Don't you see? This was in the name of science."

Tiffin spoke up, "Is that how you've justified it to yourself? That somehow killing three young women was okay because it was for science?"

North crushed the butt of his cigarette out, "Wasn't that what Dr. Mengele said as he was torturing and murdering innocent children?" He slammed his hand down on the metal table, "Wasn't it!"

"I don't know what Mengele said! I do know that you can't tie those murders to me. You have, what do you cops call it," Doolen paused as he thought, "circumstantial evidence."

"As we speak, your wife is at Memorial Hospital dying. Would you like to see her one last time?" North tone was calming.

"Of course I want to see her!"

"Tell us how you chose, kidnapped, and killed those three girls. And, tell us how you got blood to keep your wife alive while you were in Iowa."

The color drained from Doolen's face as he weighed his options. "I've loved Doris since I first laid eyes on her."

"Do you want to see her again?" Tiffin said in a near whisper.

Doolen nodded as he began to speak, "I chose each girl because they appeared to be robust, healthy, and had O-negative blood as Doris does. They each came from broken homes, which statistically meant that their quality of life and life prospects were poor. I traveled throughout Eastern Iowa and used my position as a physician to get blood from blood banks in numerous counties. I have no privileges here in Michigan, so I knew I was going to need to bring a supply with me."

"Linda, Patty, and Susan are the supply you're talking about, yes?" North asked.

"Yes, that's correct."

Tiffin looked at the doctor, "With a sick wife, why were you coming to Michigan at all?"

Doolen looked at Tiffin like he was daft, "I deserve a vacation, too, don't I?"

North shook his head, "I'm going to get a court reporter in here who will take your statement. You will tell her exactly what you just told us as I ask you questions. Once that's done, we'll take you to see your wife. Understood?"

Doolen nodded his consent.

The headline on the LaSalle Palladium Sunday morning read, "SAND RABBIT MURDERER CAUGHT!" The subhead read, "Macabre Doctor Drained Blood of Victims." Chief Cummings had been correct; the wire services carried the story coast-to-coast.

Chapter 23

Tiffin hung up the phone on his desk and scratched a note on his blotter while waiting for North to arrive to work. In the two weeks since Doolen had confessed to the murders of the Iowa teens, Tiffin had been interviewed by journalists from across the country and as far away as Japan. North refused every interview.

When North finally did arrive, he was wearing a wrinkled suit and smelling of Suzette's perfume.

"Just got off the phone," Tiffin began.

North picked up the sentence, "And someone in Tibet wanted to talk to you about the vampire doctor."

"No, a body has been found out at Tin City."

"Shit, here we go again," North pulled a fresh pack of Pall Malls from his pocket and tore the cellophane wrapper off. "Do we know who the body belonged to?"

"Harry Fuchs. He was found by workers from the electric company who were out there disconnecting the power."

"Fuchs?! Damn, there goes our case against Machine Gun. Does it look like foul play?" North lit a cigarette.

"I spoke with Doc Howard; he said it appears to have been natural causes."

North pulled off his jacket and hung it over the back of his chair before he sat down, "We've still got the Chapman woman. She can testify to what she heard him say. But that's nowhere as good as Fuch's being able to testify to what Machine Gun said directly to him."

Tiffin leaned forward, "So what are we going to do?"

"We're going to let the DA figure this out." North walked over to the coffee urn and poured a cup, "What else came in overnight?"

The detectives split the message slips and began to prioritize their day. "Someone broke into the camera shop on State Street last night, and I've got two gas stations that were robbed within twenty minutes of each other," Tiffin said.

North leafed through the slips he'd taken, "A farmer reports someone stole gas from his storage tank, and a woman reported that her neighbor is watching her as she undresses."

Tiffin chuckled, "Do you suppose we're going to have to tell her to close her curtains?"

The Prosecutor for the District Attorney's office paused in front of the witness stand, "Would you please state your name and rank for the court."

"Brian Richard North. Detective lieutenant with the LaSalle Harbor Police Department."

"Will you please tell the Court what the late Harry Fuchs told you of the conversation he had with the defendant, Kelly George?"

"Objection!" George's attorney shouted. "Hearsay!"

"Sustained," the judge barked.

The prosecutor paused to collect his thoughts, "Detective North, is it your understanding that Mr. George had spoken to others about having murdered Byron Cudlip?"

"Objection!"

"Overruled," the judge looked at the prosecuting attorney, "You're on thin ice here. Tread lightly." He then nodded toward North, "You may answer the question as asked."

"Yes," North answered.

"How is it that Mr. George came to be arrested?"

"Mr. George was arrested at one-forty Christmas morning for having robbed a taxi driver."

"How did you connect that taxi robbery with the murder of Byron Cudlip?"

"We had been looking for a man who called himself Machine Gun Kelly. When we learned that a Kelly George had been arrested, we realized that Kelly might be a first name and not a surname."

The prosecutor looked at the jury as he spoke to North, "And how did you proceed?"

"My partner, Detective Barry Tiffin, and I interviewed Mr. George."

"And following that interview, what did you do?"

"We sought witnesses who could testify against George."

"Did you uncover witnesses?" the prosecutor asked.

North nodded, "Yes. Over the course of our investigation, we found three."

"Are those witnesses here in this courtroom?"

"Yes. Miss Dolly Chapman and Bobby Baxter. Mr. Harry Fuchs passed away since he was interviewed."

"Thank you, Detective. That will be all," the prosecutor walked back to his table as the defense attorney stood."

"Mr. North, at any time did my client acknowledge that he knew Mr. Cudlip?"

"Yes."

"Did my client acknowledge he killed Mr. Cudlip?"

"No, but…"

The attorney cut him off, "So, based on hearsay alone, you have railroaded my client in an attempt to pin the unfortunate murder of Mr. Cudlip on him."

North tensed, "We did no such thing."

"But, here we are. The Police Department arrested my client for a taxi robbery, a crime to which he readily admits. And you found a convenient scapegoat upon which to close an open murder case. Isn't that true, detective?"

"No," North felt his neck and shoulders tense.

"Do you have any evidence that links my client to this murder?"

"No."

The defense attorney turned to the judge, "No more questions for this witness."

The judge looked down to the witness stand, "You are excused."

North walked into the corridor outside the courtroom and lit a cigarette. Tiffin was waiting for him, "How'd it go?"

"We're screwed. The judge won't allow us to testify to what Fuchs said, and that leaves us with the testimony of a drunk and a barmaid."

The detectives were still sitting outside the courtroom when twenty minutes later, a couple of reporters ran to the payphones. North jumped up, "What's going on?"

One of the reporters looked over his shoulder as he reached for a receiver, "Dolly Chapman says she doesn't remember overhearing a conversation. The defense attorney asked for the case to be dismissed. The judge agreed."

"Come on, Tiff," North said as he crushed the Stetson onto his head, "let's go get a drink."

George ran down the courthouse stairs past North and Tiffin. Once on the sidewalk, he turned around and faced them, "You made yourself look pretty stupid in there North."

"You walked today, George. There's always tomorrow."

As the detectives walked toward the street and their car, George continued to taunt them, "You guys ain't shit, you know that? Now that the case has been thrown out because you couldn't find a way to pin it on me, I'll tell you a secret."

North ignored him as he climbed into the driver's side of the Ford. George stepped around the front of the car to follow North and into the path of a passing Producer's Creamy truck. Machine Gun was thrown thirty feet down the road; the GMC logo clearly visible on his forehead where the truck had struck him.

North lit a Pall Mall, "Sometimes justice comes in the form of a milk truck."

A sneak preview of the next Brick North Mystery

Chapter 1

The barrel of North's .38 Colt Detective Special dug into the green leather chair and pushed the leather shoulder holster in which it rode into his ribs. He adjusted the holster and his position in the chair. Chief Cummings shook his head, "Why don't you wear a holster on your belt like the other guys?"

North took a drag on the Pall Mall cigarette that hung from his lip, "I like this better. So, why did you want to see me?"

Pete Cummings smiled, which seemed counter to the Marine bearing he normally kept, "I've got a special assignment for you."

"Why don't I like the sound of that?" Brick questioned as he picked a piece of loose tobacco off his lip.

"This'll be a walk in the park," Cummings relit his pipe, "You're going to be working with the State Department as the local liaison between them, us, and a Soviet ballet company that will be performing here next week."

"Ballet company? What the hell do I know about ballet?" North retorted.

1

"I'm guessing nothing. But I'm not asking you to dance, I'm asking you to help keep these people safe while they're in our jurisdiction. You up to that, or should I find someone else?"

"I don't get it. Why do a bunch of dancers need protection?"

"Everywhere they've visited so far, they've been met with 'better dead than red' activists."

"Isn't it the State Department's job to provide protection?"

"They are, by asking us to do it for them."

"Okay, so what do I need to do?" North crushed the cigarette butt into the ashtray on Cumming's desk.

"You'll need to put a team together, check out the theater and hotel rooms before they arrive to make certain everything is good. And, while they're here, you and your team will provide security."

"And what will the State Department be doing?"

"Probably watching you watch the ballet company."

North, resigning himself to the inevitable, nodded, "Sure, what could possibly go wrong?"

www.ingramcontent.com/pod-product-compliance
Lightning Source LLC
Chambersburg PA
CBHW070106280626
47159CB00016B/1467